CW01457605

TAINTED

FRANCES
BLACKTHORN

Thank you for embarking
on this journey with me,
diving into the pages of
my imagination *FB*

"Tainted"
Copyright © 2023 by Frances Blackthorn

ALL RIGHTS RESERVED

No part of this book may be used or reproduced in any
manner whatsoever without written permission except in the
case of brief quotations embodied in critical articles and
reviews.

This is a work of fiction. Names, characters, places, and
incidents are products of the author's imagination or are used
fictitiously. Any resemblance to actual events, locales,
organizations, or persons, living or dead, is entirely
coincidental.

Published by Frances Blackthorn
First edition: 2023
Cover design copyright © 2023 by Frances Blackthorn
ISBN: 979-8-89074-903-1

www.francesblackthorn.com

TRIGGER CONTENT WARNING

Please be aware that *Tainted* contains content that may disturb or trigger some readers. The main character is a killer, and the story includes graphic violence, explicit sexual content, knife violence, visual depictions of blood, murder, and physical harm.

If you are sensitive to any of the above topics, *please proceed with caution*. This story is intended for mature audiences only and may not be suitable for all readers.

Please prioritize your mental health and well-being while reading this book. If at any point you feel uncomfortable or distressed, please take a break and seek support from a trusted friend or professional.

Remember, it is okay to put down a book if it is causing you distress or negatively affecting your mental health. *Your well-being is the most important thing.*

Thank you for reading, and I hope you enjoy the story

PROLOGUE

I'm here for one reason only: *to protect Alina Moskal*.

So, here I am, standing in this gilded cage, waiting for the next shot to ring out.

It's a familiar feeling, blood stench, and death's cold touch.

But this time, it's different.

This time, *I'm not the predator*.

I'm the protector.

The one responsible for keeping Alina safe. And I won't let anything stand in my way.

The ballroom is packed with people dressed in their finest clothes and dripping with diamonds and gold. I scan the room, my eyes moving from one face to the next, searching for any sign of danger.

That's when I see him.

A man in a black suit, his face obscured by shadows. He's watching her, his eyes tracking her every move. I move towards him, my hand going to the gun at my waist. He doesn't move, doesn't even flinch when I approach. I know what he is.

Another killer hired to ruin the Moskal family.

Before I can make a move, the lights go out. The ballroom is plunged into darkness, the sound of screams and gunfire echoing through the room. I can hear Alina's voice screaming in fear. I turn and run towards her, my heart pounding with the need to protect her at all costs.

I see her silhouette in the darkness. A frightened figure lost amidst the chaos. My instincts take over, and I move towards her, careful to remain hidden from view. As I draw near, I can see the fear in her eyes, the desperation etched on her face.

The chaos is overwhelming, the screams and gunfire mingling into a deafening cacophony. But I keep my focus. My senses heightened as I navigate through the shadows. I can feel the presence of the other killer lurking somewhere in the darkness.

But I'm ready for him.

I'm a killer.

I am a predator.

And I won't let him hurt her.

Not on my watch.

CHAPTER ONE

Nikolai Moskal's office is quiet except for his fingers tapping against the polished wooden desk. I stand before him, my arms crossed over my chest, waiting for him to speak.

"I'm sure you know why you are here," he says, his gaze piercing me. "I have a job for you."

I nod but remain silent.

"My daughter's life is in danger. There have been threats made against her, and I need someone I can trust to protect her," he continues.

"And you think that someone is me."

"You are one of the best killers I've ever met," he says, "I know I can trust you with my daughter's life."

I don't flinch at his words.

I'm used to being hired to kill, protect, and do whatever it takes to get the job done.

"I don't need to remind you what will happen if something happens to my daughter, Kane," he continues. "I'm sure you understand the consequences."

"I understand, Mr. Moskal," I keep my voice steady.

"Good," he leans back in his chair. "You start tonight. Alina will be attending a charity ball. You will be her bodyguard for the night."

"Is there anything else I need to know?"

"Just keep her safe," he replies sharply. "And remember, if you fail, it won't just be her life on the line. It will be yours too."

I nod, turning to leave.

"Kane," he calls out, and I pause. "Don't forget whom you are working for."

I turn to face him, "I won't."

I leave Moskal's office, feeling the world's weight settle on my shoulders. It's a familiar sensation, the burden of responsibility that comes with the job.

If I fail in my mission, it won't just be her life on the line. *It will be mine too.*

My eyes catch a glimpse of a figure in the corridor. A beautiful young woman with honey-blonde hair and agate eyes stands before me, blocking my path. For a split second, I freeze.

It's Alina Moskal. This girl's life is in my hands.

As I step forward, my gaze lingers on the way Alina's body curves in all the right places, her black silk dress hugging her like a second skin. Her lips part as I brush past her, the heat of her body radiating against mine. The scent of her perfume hits me like a ton of bricks, and my mind starts to wander to dark, *forbidden places.*

I feel Alina's eyes on my back. I can practically hear the questions in her head.

Who am I?

Why am I here?

And most importantly, *can she trust me?*

The answer to that last question is simple.

No one can be trusted in this game.

I hear Nikolai's voice calling out for Alina from his office, and I quicken my pace. I don't need any more distractions. *The sooner I complete this mission, the sooner I can leave and forget that I ever crossed paths with Alina Moskal.*

•

Protecting Alina Moskal won't be an easy job. It will require constant vigilance and a level of proximity that I'm only somewhat comfortable with.

The Moskal family is no ordinary client.

They are powerful.

They are ruthless.

They have countless enemies who would stop at nothing to get to them. Getting involved with them is a risk I'm not sure I'm willing to take

But the paycheck is too good to pass up.

I return to my apartment and begin to pack my things. My duffel bag is filled with only the essentials: weapons, ammunition, clothes, and personal items I can't bear to leave behind.

The apartment has a worn, lived-in feel to it, with furniture that's seen better days. The walls are painted a neutral color, but a few posters and pictures are hung up to add some personality to the space. The bedroom is sparsely furnished, with just a bed and a dresser, but it's cozy and comfortable. The kitchen is tiny, with a small fridge and a microwave, but it's enough for my needs.

I take a photo of my sister before leaving.

Klara is the only family I have left, even though I have no idea where she is.

Or if she is even alive.

I remember the cold, unfeeling eyes of the men who broke into our home, their guns pointed at us as we huddled together in fear. *Our parents were brutally murdered that night.*

The men who invaded our home *had no mercy.*

No compassion.

They ripped our family apart, leaving us shattered and alone. I tried to protect Klara, but I was overpowered, and I watched in horror as they took our parents away from us.

After that night, my sister and I were ripped apart and sent in separate ways.

I searched for her everywhere.

She was nowhere to be found.

The thought of her out there, alone and vulnerable, haunted me every single day. I vowed never to let anyone make me feel that way again, and so I became the man I am today: *cold, ruthless, and unfeeling.*

•

I return to the Moskal mansion, and the gates open as soon as I approach. The security is tight, and I can see why.

The mansion is massive, with multiple levels, gardens, and a pool. *It's not exactly the best place for a family that wants to keep a low profile*, and it's also the perfect place for danger to lurk around every corner.

As I enter the mansion, I'm greeted by Nikolai Moskal. His voice echoes in the foyer, his words formal and stilted. "Kane, welcome to our home."

"Thank you, Mr. Moskal." I reply, my eyes scanning the room. The Moskal family has enemies willing to wait and bide their time until the right moment to strike.

Nikolai leads me to my room, which is located on the first floor. It's a spacious suite with a king-sized bed, a desk, and a balcony overlooking the gardens. There's a closet where I can hang my clothes and a dresser to store my weapons.

"I hope this room meets your needs," Nikolai says, "We take security very seriously here and expect the same from you."

I nod, "I'll do everything I can to keep Alina safe."

"I will be counting on you, Kane."

I've been in this business for years and have never been hired to protect anyone. It's always been the opposite, actually.

I'm usually the one doing the killing.

This mission will be more complicated than anything I've ever done before. *But I know I must succeed.*

CHAPTER TWO

I take my time settling into my new room and unpack everything I'll need for tonight. That's when I hear footsteps behind me, and I turn around to see Alina standing in the doorway, her eyes scanning my body with curiosity.

"Are you the babysitter?" she asks sarcastically.

I raise an eyebrow. "Something like that."

"Well, I don't need a babysitter," she says, stepping closer. "I can take care of myself."

"Good to know," my eyes roam over her body. "But I'm not just here to babysit."

"Then why are you here?"

I step closer to her until we're standing only inches apart. "Let's just say I have a job to do."

"Is that so?" she smirks, looking at me through her lashes. "And what kind of job requires you to follow me around like a lost puppy?"

I narrow my eyes at her, not amused by her teasing. "The kind that pays well."

She chuckles, and her eyes shine with mischief. "Well, I hope my father is paying you enough to put up with me," she steps closer. "I can be a handful, you know."

I stand my ground, not giving in to her teasing. "I can handle it."

"We will see about that," she says, "I feel you might just be in over your head with me, Kane."

Of course, she already knows my name.

"I doubt that," I say, "I'm not easily intimidated."

Her lips curve into a wicked grin. "Is that so?" she steps closer until our bodies almost touch. "Well, I guess we'll just have to find out, won't we?"

Without another word, I turn back to my belongings, feeling Alina's eyes on me as I move. I can sense her lingering in the doorway.

"You look like trouble," she says.

"That's because I am," I simply respond, my voice cold.

Alina's smile grows wider, and she walks to me, pressing her body against mine. I can feel her warmth through the thin fabric of her dress, and I fight the urge to reach out and touch her.

"Maybe I like trouble," she says, her breath hot, touching my neck.

I remain silent as I study her.

Alina's boldness is a dangerous game.

And I don't intend to fall for it.

She leans in closer, and I can't help but notice how her body curves against mine.

The way her scent fills my nostrils.

My primal part, which craves danger and excitement, stirs to life.

"Alina, what are you doing?"

"Just welcoming you home."

I take a step back, breaking the contact between us. "I didn't come here for a welcome party," I say, my voice hardening.

However, she doesn't seem deterred and steps closer to me again. "Then what did you come here for besides babysitting me?"

"That's none of your concern."

She reaches up to trace her fingers down my chest, and a jolt of electricity runs through me. I grab her wrist, holding it firmly in place.

"I wouldn't if I were you," I warn her.

She looks up at me, her eyes wide, and I know I've caught her off guard. For a moment, we stand in place, looking at each other.

Then, as if breaking the spell, she pulls her hand away and steps back.

"Fine," she says coldly, "I guess I will see you around."

And with that, she turns and walks away.

As soon as Alina disappears from view, I release a breath I hadn't realized I was holding. Her flirtatious and provocative behavior had stirred something deep inside me.

Something that I usually keep under strict control.

Maybe it's her confidence.

Her boldness.

The refusal to play by the rules.

There's a fire in her eyes that I've never seen before, *it's dangerous and tempting*, and I feel myself getting pulled deeper and deeper into her orbit.

But I can't let that happen.

Alina is Nikolai's daughter.

I'm here to protect her.

I finish unpacking and prepare to take a quick shower, trying to wash away these thoughts.

The steam fills the bathroom, and I feel my mind slipping back to Alina and the tension between us.

Fuck, this wasn't supposed to be happening, Kane.

The darkness that consumes me takes over, and I allow myself a moment of relaxation to indulge in my desires.

I shake my head, trying to clear my mind, but the images become more vivid. The heat of the water mixes with the heat building inside me, and I can feel my desire growing stronger.

My hand brushes against my length, and I groan at the sensation. I lean against the wall, my forehead pressed against the cool tiles, as I slowly stroke myself.

Her curves are dangerous,
Her skin is smooth and flawless.

I long to run my hands over her soft skin, to feel her body arch and writhe beneath mine. I imagine tracing the curve of her hipbone with my finger, feeling the heat of her skin beneath my touch.

The images of Alina become even more intense, and I can feel myself nearing the edge. But I force myself to stop, not wanting to give in to my primal urges.

I step out of the shower and wrap a towel around my waist, my long hair still dripping wet. I run my fingers through the strands, pulling them back into a tight bun at the nape of my neck.

I take my time getting dressed, carefully selecting each piece of clothing, considering the need for comfort and mobility.

The black tuxedo covering the tattoos that adorn my entire body is a necessary camouflage, allowing me to blend in with the other partygoers.

I slide on form-fitting black pants, then slip into a black turtleneck. The fabric feels soft against my skin, and I can't help but appreciate the way it clings to my muscles.

Next, I strap on my weapons.

A pair of sleek, silver pistols, loaded and ready for action, and a knife are hidden in compartments under my jacket. I check each one, making sure they are fully loaded and easily accessible in case of emergency.

The weight of the weapons nestled against my chest. *I can't afford to let my guard down.*

CHAPTER THREE

I make my way through the crowd. My steps are measured and purposeful.

I can't draw attention to myself.

I'm here to blend in and keep a watchful eye on Alina from the shadows.

The ballroom is grand, with chandeliers hanging from the high ceilings and elegant decor at every turn. I feel out of place but remind myself that it's necessary for the mission.

I scan the room, searching for Alina. It takes me a few moments to spot her - she's surrounded by a group of people, her laughter ringing above the chatter. Her red dress hugs her curves, and how her hair falls in loose waves around her shoulders.

I make my way closer, but I keep my distance.

I can't risk being seen with her...

Not when so many people surround her.

Instead, I position myself near a pillar, leaning casually against it as I watch her.

Her father's bodyguard, Stian, is nearby; I can tell he's on high alert. I nod at him in acknowledgment, but I don't approach. I need to maintain a low profile if I'm going to keep Alina safe.

I watch as she dances with a man in a tuxedo, her movements graceful and fluid while his hand rests on her waist possessively. My jaw clenches as I imagine what he must be thinking as he touches her fragile body.

I can see how her body moves in time with the music, her hips swaying seductively as she dances with the other man, and I know it's not my place to care.

Suddenly, a voice breaks through my thoughts, distracting me from the scene before me. "Excuse me, sir, may I help you with something?" a waiter asks, holding a tray of drinks.

I turn to him, taking a deep breath to steady myself. "No, thank you," I reply, my eyes quickly flicking back to Alina.

But when I turn back to the spot where she was dancing, *she is gone*. My heart rate spikes, and I scan the room frantically, trying to spot her in the crowd.

"Excuse me, sir?" the waiter says again, trying to get my attention.

"Not now," I snap, focusing entirely on finding Alina.

Finally, I spot her across the room.

Her back turned to me as the other man's hand drifts lower, dangerously close to the curve of her hips.

Watching the other man's hand go down, my body reacts without my permission. My breathing becomes shallow, my heart pounding, and my fingers curl into fists at my sides.

I want to rip his hand off.

I can't help but imagine how his hand feels against her skin, the heat of his palm as it glides down her waist, and how his fingers dig into her soft flesh.

She breaks away from the man's embrace and makes her way toward me, a sly smile playing at the corners of her lips.

"Enjoying the view?" she asks.

I turn to meet her gaze, holding her in a heated stare. "You shouldn't be seen with me," I warn.

"I saw you watching me," she says, her smile growing wider. "I didn't realize you were into that kind of thing."

"I'm not sure what you're talking about," I glance around us, and scan the crowd for potential threats.

She steps closer to me, her body almost touching mine, "Don't pretend," she whispers, her breath hot against my ear. "I saw the way you were looking at me. I'm just unsure if you were enjoying or not seeing me with another man's hands on my body."

My mind races as I try to keep my composure while I keep my eyes on her, trying to read her expression, but she keeps her gaze fixed on mine, a challenge in her eyes.

"You have no idea what you're talking about."

Alina leans closer, her lips brushing against my ear as she speaks. "Oh, I think I do," she teases. "I saw the way your eyes followed every curve of my body, the way you were practically drooling over me." She pulls back slightly, a mischievous glint in her eye.

I take a step back, trying to create some distance between us. "You are playing with fire," I warn her, "Don't push me, Alina."

A sultry sound leaves her body as she laughs. "I like it when you get all intense," she says, "It's so sexy."

"You have no idea who I am, Alina," I warn her.

"Show me, then, Kane." She challenges.

A stir of activity captures the center of the ballroom, and my attention is drawn to the gathering crowd, their voices reduced to a murmur of anticipation. A man steps onto the stage, and the room instantly falls silent. I observe as he begins to speak, his voice projecting across the ballroom, drawing my focus away from Alina's gaze.

"Thank you all for coming tonight," he begins, his words smooth and practiced. "I'm honored to see so many familiar faces in the crowd, and I want to take a moment to express my gratitude to all of you."

I watch the guests nod in agreement, some clapping politely.

"But I want to remind you all that we are here for a greater purpose," the guy continues, "There are forces at work that threaten to tear our community apart, to destroy the very fabric of our society. It's up to us to stand strong against them, to protect what we hold dear."

The man keeps talking for some minutes before looking at Alina, "Our beloved Alina Moskal has something she would like to share with us all. Alina, would you please come to the stage?"

The crowd begins to murmur in excitement as Alina slowly approaches the stage. As I follow her with my eyes, I see a figure lurking in the shadows, watching her intently.

He looks out of place like he doesn't belong here.

Instinctively, I touch the gun at my side, ensuring it's easily accessible - my mind races with the possibilities of what this guy could be planning.

My heart pounds in my chest as the man puts his hand into his pocket.

I step forward.

My eyes fix on him as I try to get a better look at his face.

The lights go out, and the ballroom is plunged into darkness. I move quickly and silently through the shadows, my senses on high alert. The chaos around me is overwhelming, but I focus solely on finding and keeping Alina safe. The screams and gunfire are deafening, and I can hear the distinct sound of a struggle somewhere nearby.

As I navigate through the darkness, I catch a glimpse of movement out of the corner of my eye. I turn, gun at the ready, and see the faint outline of a figure.

It's him.

I move towards the man, my steps silent as I close the distance. He turns towards me, surprised to see me so close. At that moment, I see the recognition in his eyes. *He knows who I am.*

We engage in a fierce struggle, the darkness making it difficult to see.

But I'm a killer.

I was trained to do this.

I use all my skills to overpower him, finally landing a crushing blow that sends him to the ground. He lies there, unmoving, as I catch my breath, quickly reach into my pocket, and retrieve a small knife. It's slick in my hand, the blade glinting in the dim light. I slide the knife across the man's throat, feeling the resistance of flesh and muscle. It's a swift, efficient motion, and the man gasps and shudders before going still. I wipe the blade on his shirt, careful not to leave any evidence behind.

I need to find Alina to make sure she's safe.

My hand slips the knife back into my pocket as I close my jacket to conceal any bloodstains.

I move cautiously through the screams. I know there are more of them out there, waiting for their chance to strike.

As I round the corner, I come face to face with another one of them. He's holding a gun, his finger poised on the trigger. We stare at each other for a moment, sizing up the competition.

I don't give him a chance to make the first move. I launch myself at him, throwing him off balance with a swift kick to the knee.

He staggers back.

But I don't let up.

I strike him hard in the gut, feeling the satisfying crunch of bone under my fist.

Blood is dripping down his face as he tries to fight back, but I'm too quick. I dodge his blows and land another punch connecting with his jaw. He falls to the ground, writhing in pain.

I'm about to finish him off when I hear the sound of footsteps.

More of them are coming.

I need to move quickly.

I retrieve my gun and take off down the hallway, my senses on high alert.

I move through the shadows, trying to find Alina's voice.

And finally, I see her.

I approach her and touch her shoulder gently, making her jump, facing me. I take her hand, pull her close, and run toward the exit. The chaos around us is overwhelming, with screams filling the air.

But I keep moving, focusing on getting Alina out of here.

We burst out of the ballroom into the night air, the cold hitting us like a brick wall. I can see our car parked in the distance, and I pull her along, slowing down when we reach it. I open the door and help her in before entering the driver's seat.

I glance at her as I start the car and pull away from the curb. She's still shaking, her breathing ragged.

But she's alive, and that's all that matters.

CHAPTER FOUR

I park the car a few miles from the ball, and Alina stays silent inside as I take the call.

I hear Stian's flat voice on the other end, and my gut tightens.

"Is Nikolai okay?" I ask.

"He's alive and well," Stian confirms.

I let out a breath, "What are his orders?"

"Take Alina home and keep her safe," He replies coldly.

I can hear the underlying threat behind his words, and I know Nikolai's orders are not to be taken lightly. "And what about you and Nikolai?"

"We have business to attend to," Stian says flatly.

I nod, even though he can't see me. "Understood."

As I end the call, I can sense Alina's eyes on me. "What's going on?"

"It's not safe for you to be out here."

"That doesn't answer my question."

I sigh, "Your father's orders are for me to take you home and keep you safe."

"Why? What happened?" she presses.

"I don't have the details," I reply, my tone final.

We fall into silence as I drive towards her estate.

But I feel her eyes on me...
Burning into my skin.

"You are not the one to make anything easy, are you?" Alina snaps, breaking the silence.

"I'm not here to make things easy," I keep focusing on the road.

"You are always so damn cold."

"I'm not paid to be warm and friendly,"

"Can you at least try to be a little less stone-faced and a little more...human?"

"Never said I was human,"

"You're lucky you're hot."

I shoot her a sideways glance, "I'm also not paid to be hot," I reply, "So do us both a favor and shut up."

Her mouth snaps shut, and for a moment, the only sound in the car is the engine's hum.

I leave the car and slam the door shut when we arrive at the mansion. I don't glance to see if she's following me.

She stays in the car for a moment, and I return to her door, standing there with my arms crossed. "If you think I'm going to open the door for you, you are very much mistaken, princess. I'm not your servant."

She rolls her eyes at my words but opens the door and steps out of the car, her expensive gown rustling with each step. "Whatever," she mutters, but I ignore her and lead the way inside the house.

Once we are inside, I quickly look around to ensure everything is secure before turning to face her. "I need to check your room."

"What, you don't trust me?"

"I don't trust anyone."

"Fine," she says, gesturing towards the stairs. "Upstairs, second door on the left."

I follow her up the stairs, and when we reach her room I step inside, my eyes scanning the area for any signs of a break-in or disturbance.

I keep my expression blank as Alina leans against the doorframe, watching me with a sultry smirk on her lips. "Do you like what you see, Kane?"

"I'm finished here."

I leave her room and go to my own.

•

I step into the shower and let the hot water wash away the blood from my skin. *The sensation of the water beating against my chest is pure bliss.*

Suddenly, the bathroom door opens, and my eyes snap open to see Alina standing outside the clear shower door. "What are you doing here?" I keep my voice as steady as possible.

"I couldn't resist," she says, "Seeing you in the shower, all wet and steamy...I couldn't help myself."

I raise an eyebrow, feeling both aroused and irritated at her sudden appearance.

Shit, this woman...

"You shouldn't be here."

I quickly grab a towel and wrap it around my waist, trying to hide my arousal. I open the door and move to step out of the shower, but Alina pushes me back inside, the water cascading over both of us now, wetting her dress and the towel wrapped around my waist.

I protest, "Alina, if your father finds out you are here, he will have my head and yours."

Alina places a finger on my lips, silencing me. "He won't find out," she whispers, "Are you afraid of my father?"

I chuckle, my gaze never leaving hers. "I'm not afraid of many things, but I don't feel like going down just because a horny girl wants to play."

Alina laughs, "Is that so?" she says, and with a flick of her wrist, her dress slips off her body, revealing her black lace panties and full breasts.

I step back, my towel slipping from my waist, "That's a dangerous game, princess," I advise.

Alina stands on tiptoe, her breasts pressing against my chest, "Maybe I like games," she whispers.

I grab her waist and pull her closer, my lips inches from hers before she crashes them against mine in a frenzy of need.

This girl will end up getting me killed.

Alina's tongue explores my mouth, igniting a wildfire of longing within me.

She's dangerous.

She's untamed.

She's everything I shouldn't want.

She's a wild card.

She's unpredictable.

She's reckless.

And I'm playing with fire by indulging in her desires.

As she presses herself closer, her hands roaming over my wet skin, I can't bring myself to care about the consequences anymore.

I want her more than I've ever wanted anything right now. And I'll deal with the fallout later.

I lift her, her legs wrapping around my waist as I press her against the cold tile wall. Her moans grow louder, the sound echoing off the bathroom walls as my lips move down her soft skin, trailing a path of fire, kissing my way from her neck to her breasts.

I take one of her hard nipples into my mouth, swirling my tongue around it while my hand massages the other breast. Her breath hitches as she arches her back, pressing her chest against me.

I suck harder, nibbling on her sensitive flesh, making her gasp in pleasure.

I feel her body trembling with desire as I switch to her other breast, taking it into my mouth and giving it the same attention.

The taste of her skin.

The feel of her body against mine.

It's all too much to resist.

Her nails dig into my back, urging me on, and I feel myself losing control.

As I retake her lips, my hands slide down her back and grip her firmly behind, pulling her closer. Alina lets out a soft gasp, her body shivering with pleasure. I want to feel her skin against mine, so I pull at her panties, tearing them off her body with desperate need.

Her body is intoxicating, and I can't get enough of her.

Her body arches towards mine, seeking more of my touch. My fingers find their way between her legs, and she lets out a guttural moan.

I take her hand and guide it toward my hardening arousal. Her fingers wrap around me, eliciting a low groan from my lips.

I want to take her right here and right now.

But I can't.

Not yet.

"Kane," she whispers, "Please, take me. I need you."

I pull away, "Not yet, princess," I growl. "I want to savor every moment with you." I close the water and guide her towards the bed.

She lies down, and I crawl on top of her, again taking her lips.

Our bodies are a tangled mess of desire, and as the heat between us intensifies, I know that I can't resist her any longer. I enter her with my fingers, feeling her tightness envelop me, and she cries out in ecstasy.

"Take me, Kane," she asks again.

"I said 'no,'"

She doesn't listen and takes control.

Her hands roam over my chest, and before I can even register what's happening, *Alina's lips are on mine*, her tongue exploring every inch of my mouth. Her hands reach my length, and she begins to stroke me, her touch firm.

I groan as she takes me into her mouth, her tongue swirling around the tip before she takes me deeper, her lips tight around me. I grip the sheets as she moves up and down, the sensation almost too much to bear.

I want to flip her over and take over, but something about her taking charge is too much of a turn-on to resist.

I watch as she continues to please me.

Her eyes are locked on mine.

And I know I'm entirely at her mercy.

She takes me deeper and deeper, and I feel my body tightening, ready to release.

But I don't want to come yet.

I want to touch her.

All of her.

I sit up, pulling her with me, and I take her lips with mine, tasting myself on her tongue. My hands find their way to her breasts, teasing her nipples until they're hard.

With a flick of my wrist, I flip us over, pinning her beneath me.

I trail kisses down her neck...

Over her chest...

And my hand finds its way between her legs.

She's already wet and ready for me.

I grow harder as I explore her with my fingers. I want to taste every inch of her, to make her come undone beneath me.

As she moans and writhes beneath me, I know I can't hold back any longer. I flip her around so she's straddling me, facing the opposite direction. I guide her back down onto my length, and she moans as her mouth takes me in. I feel her hands on my thighs, her head thrown back as I thrust into her.

I lean forward, my tongue finding its way to her clit, and I start to flick and suck, my movements in sync with my thrusts.

Her moans become louder, the sound of her pleasure filling the room. I can feel myself getting closer, knowing I won't be able to hold back for much longer.

I grip her hips, guiding her movements, and we ride the waves together until we both become undone.

CHAPTER FIVE

I wake up to Alina tracing her fingers over my back tattoos. My skin prickles with awareness, and I sit up abruptly, throwing her off balance.

"What the fuck are you doing?" I growl, turning to face her. Her eyes sparkle with amusement, and I feel my jaw clenching.

"Isn't your job to be close to me, to protect me from evil?" she taunts, crawling closer to me on the bed. "Or did I misunderstand what being my bodyguard meant?"

Shit, Kane. What have you done? This was not part of your job... at all.

"My job is to ensure you're not killed, not to fuck you," I snap.

I don't need the distraction of her tempting body clouding my judgment.

"Get the hell out of my room, Alina."

She sits up on the bed, and her eyes are still trained on me, "You are no fun," she pouts. "You were moaning just minutes ago, and now you are acting like you don't even want me near you."

"Sorry to break it to you, but I don't get attached," I tell her coldly. "Let's see what happened as the consolation prize for killing someone at the ball. Nothing more."

"You killed someone?" she asks, her eyes revealing nothing of her feelings.

I nod, not breaking eye contact with her. "What do you think the blood was?"

The memory of the kill still fresh in my mind, the adrenaline rush still coursing through my veins.

Alina recoils slightly...

As if realizing for the first time the kind of man she's dealing with.

"I told you, you don't know me, Alina," I say, "You don't know what I'm capable of. Get out now before you find out the hard way."

She stands up from the bed, facing me with fierce determination. "You think you scare me, Kane?" she challenges. "You don't know what I've been through, what I'm capable of. So don't think you can push me around and treat me like some disposable toy."

"I don't care what you've been through," I tell her, "But you need to understand one thing. I am not your friend. I am not your lover. I am your bodyguard, and my job is to keep you alive. Nothing more."

Alina's defiance only serves to stoke the fire of my anger. She grabs her clothes and storms out of the room, but not before throwing a parting shot at me.

"Fine," she spits, "But don't think I'm just going to roll over and let you walk all over me, Kane. I'm not that kind of girl." As she lingers in the doorway, she turns back to me and fires off one more question, "Why did you go ahead with me as you did?"

I feel the urge to lash out at her, but instead, I give her the only answer that comes to mind. "You have a nice pair of tits."

Alina's face falls.

I know I've hit a nerve.

But I don't care.

I grab my boxers and pull them on, my eyes never leaving hers. "Just leave, Alina," I command. "And stay away from me. The last thing I need is you getting in the way of my job."

Alina slams the door shut, leaving me alone in my room with nothing but her footsteps fading away.

You are so stupid, Kane.

Really not clever to have relations with a Moskal.

I sit on the edge of the bed, running my hand over my face as I try to get my thoughts in order.

What the hell was I thinking?

Nikolai is not a forgiving man.

He doesn't tolerate any disobedience...

If he finds out what I've done, he'll make me pay in the most brutal way possible.

He is a man of power...

And he doesn't hesitate to wield it like a weapon.

He rules his empire with an iron fist...

And anyone who dares to cross him will suffer the consequences.

I can almost feel the bones in my body shattering under the force of his men's blows, the agonizing pain ripping through my flesh as I scream for mercy that will never come.

My mind conjures images of Nikolai's cold, merciless gaze as he looks down on me, reveling in my suffering. I can almost hear his voice, commanding his men to inflict even more pain upon me.

He would enjoy making an example out of me, punishing me for my disobedience, and daring to touch his daughter.

The room feels suffocating.

I grab my shirt and pants and quickly dress, trying to ignore the lingering scent of Alina on my skin.

The temptation to go to her...

To drown in her body...

It's overwhelming.

But if Nikolai finds out, there will be no escape.

No mercy.

Only pain and death.

•

It's 3 AM sharp, and I hear the door open and close. Stian's voice, low and gravelly, reaches my ears. "Boss wants to see you in his office."

I nod, wondering what Nikolai could want from me at this hour, but I follow Stian to Nikolai's office.

Stian and I look pretty alike, physically speaking. We are both tall, muscular, and have inked bodies, but our eyes are different, even though we both have light-colored eyes - *his are a piercing blue, while mine are a steely gray*. We share the same blond hair, but while my hair is long and messy, Stian's is short and styled.

It's like Nikolai has a type.

Nikolai sits behind his desk, looking every inch the ruthless leader that he is. "Kane, you did a great job protecting Alina tonight. I'm impressed."

I nod again without a word.

He leans forward, his eyes fixed on mine. "The body they found was taken care of, but the other one wasn't quite dead yet. I have an extra job for you."

My blood runs cold at his words.

I ended up not killing the second guy.

"What do you need me to do?"

"I need you to go with Stian to handle that little problem. And take Alina with you."

I can't help the surprise that flickers across my face. This job sounds violent and different from what I thought Nikolai would want Alina to see. "Are you sure?"

Nikolai narrows his eyes at me. "Are you trying to defy my orders?"

"No, of course not," I reply quickly, "But, sir, I thought Alina's safety was our top priority. I'm not sure taking her with us is a good idea."

Nikolai leans back in his chair, "Alina is no princess. She's been around violence her whole life. She won't be bothered by it."

I nod, even though his words don't reassure me.

I don't have a choice in the matter.

I need to do what Nikolai asks of me.

I make my way up the stairs and to her room. The room is dimly lit, the only source of light coming from the moon shining through the window. Without bothering to knock, I push open the door and step inside.

And there she is...

Lying on her bed...

Fast asleep.

She's only wearing her white lace underwear, and I can't help but appreciate how her back curves and butt look in that position.

I stand there momentarily, taking in every inch of her body. Her skin is smooth and flawless, and the lace of her underwear barely covers her. Her blonde hair is spread across the pillow, and her face is peaceful in sleep.

I can see the rise and fall of her chest with every breath she takes...

... and it's mesmerizing.

I can't stay here and admire her all night.

I have a job to do.

I need to wake her up.

I make my way to the light and turn it on, "Wake up. We need to go."

She stirs and slowly opens her eyes, looking up at me in confusion. It takes a moment for her to register what's happening, but then she sits up, rubbing the sleep from her eyes. "What's going on?"

"You need to get dressed."

"Why? What's happening?"

"I don't have time to tell you that right now. Just get dressed," I repeat.

"I can't just go with you like this. I need to know what's going on," she protests, sitting up and pulling the sheets up to cover herself.

"You don't have a choice. You can either get dressed, or I'll take you from this bed and carry you to the car just like that."

She looks at me for a moment, defiance in her eyes, but then she sighs and gets out of bed.

"Fine. I'll get dressed," she says, resigned.

"You have exactly two minutes," I say, turning around and leaving the room.

I go down the stairs and head straight to the front door, knowing Stian is already waiting for us outside. I see him leaning against his car, looking impatient as he checks his watch. Alina follows me, fully dressed and ready to go. I open the door and motion for her to hurry up.

Stian gets behind the wheel, and I sit beside him while Alina sits in the back. I give her a cold glance through the rearview mirror.

Stian drives us toward our destination, and the silence in the car is only broken by the sound of the engine. I focus on the task, reviewing the plan in my mind, and *Alina remains silent*.

We arrive at the location, and I step out of the car, my eyes scanning the surroundings.

Everything seems in order, so I signal Alina to follow me.

We walk inside the abandoned building. The smell of dust and decay fills the air, and I can feel Alina's hesitation behind me. I turn around to face her and give her a stern look. "Stay close," I command before turning back around and continuing.

We go down a long hallway until we reach a room at the end. Inside, we find the man I left alive at the ball, tied to a chair, in a terrible state.

His face is bruised and swollen.

His eyes barely open.
And blood drips from his nose and mouth.
I approach the man, looking him in the eyes.
Alina doesn't even flinch.
This is just a necessary step to tie up loose ends.
"You should have stayed dead," I say as I approach the man.

CHAPTER SIX

I approach the man, and Stian takes his place behind me. We exchange a nod, silently agreeing to what's about to happen. The man's eyes dart back and forth between us, his breathing ragged and uneven.

I grab his chin, forcing him to look at me.

His pupils are dilated, and sweat beads on his forehead.

"You thought you could plot to destroy the Moskal family and get away with it," I say.

His Adam's apple bobs as he swallows hard.

But he doesn't say a word.

I let go of his chin and step back, allowing Stian to take over. He viciously punishes the man's stomach, causing him to gasp for air.

Blood dribbles down his chin.

But Stian isn't done.

He grabs a nearby pipe and starts hitting the man with it repeatedly. The sound of metal against flesh echoes throughout the room.

I see the fear in the man's eyes, and I can feel the adrenaline coursing through my veins. I take a deep breath and step forward, delivering a punch to his already battered face. Blood spurts from his nose, mixing with the blood already coating his face.

The man tries to speak, but all that comes out is a gurgling noise. I hit him again and again, my fists connecting with his face, stomach, and ribs. He crumples to the ground, wheezing and gasping for breath.

Stian tosses the pipe aside and steps back, breathing heavily. The room is filled with the sound of the man's labored breathing and the smell of blood and sweat. I look down at him, his face a bloody mess, and I feel a sense of satisfaction wash over me.

Alina remains silent.

Her expression still blank.

Finally, I step back, breathing heavily.

The man's face is a bloody mess, his body limp and broken. I signal to Stian to take care of the body, and I leave the room, Alina following silently behind me.

Alina finally speaks up. "Was that guy at the ball to kill me?"

"Yes, he was," I reply bluntly.

Alina's eyes narrow slightly as though she's processing the information. "Why? What do they want from me?"

I don't waste time with pleasantries. "They want what your family has, Alina. Your wealth, your power, your influence. You were just an obstacle in their way."

"And how many more of them are there?"

"We are not sure," I reply, "But we know others will stop at nothing to get what they want."

"Why did you take me with you to take care of him?" she finally asks.

The old man's orders are crystal clear.
Protect his daughter at all costs.

But why he made her come with Stian and me to the middle of nowhere to beat a guy up is beyond me.

I hesitate for a moment, considering how much I should tell her. "I need you close to me, Alina," I say, "I can't let you out of my sight, not even for a moment. You need to be under my protection 24/7. Those are my orders."

It's not a lie...
But it's not the whole truth, either.

Alina doesn't protest. Instead, she nods, and her expression resigns.

We continue down our way to the car in silence, and the only sound is the echo of our footsteps.

I know for sure her eyes are on me.

But I don't look back.

I don't owe her an explanation.

And I don't plan on giving her one.

As we reach the car, Alina stops abruptly, making me turn to face her. Her eyes are searching, but I keep my expression blank. "I need to know, Kane," she says, "Can I trust you?"

"No," I say, meeting her gaze. "That would be pretty stupid of you."

I open the car door and slide inside, not bothering to check if she follows.

•

As we make our way back to the mansion, Alina runs up to her room while Stian and I head to Nikolai's office. My hand hovers over the doorknob, and I push open the heavy wooden door to reveal Nikolai seated at his desk. The room is dimly lit, and Stian positions himself in front of the door to guard the entrance.

"What's the news?" Nikolai asks, his voice gruff.

I don't waste any time. "He's no longer a problem."

Nikolai nods, a satisfied smile playing on his lips. "And what about her?" his tone suggests he's referring to his daughter.

"She's safe."

Nikolai's smile widens, and he leans back in his chair. "Excellent work, Kane," he says. "You've once again proven your worth to the family."

I nod, not really feeling the satisfaction that I should.

I can't shake the memory of Alina's indifferent expression after witnessing violence earlier.

I know I shouldn't question Nikolai's decisions, but...

I take a deep breath, "Mr. Moskal, forgive me for asking, but..."

Nikolai's face darkens, his smile vanishing in a heartbeat as he interrupts me. "Kane, you know your place," he says with a sharp edge to his voice. "Don't question my orders."

Stian's gaze is razor-sharp, boring into me as I backpedal. "Of course, Mr. Moskal."

I spin on my heel and make a beeline for the door, the sound of Nikolai's muted voice following me out.

Stian trails me with his eyes as I depart, but we don't speak.

We both know our place in this world.

Questioning Nikolai's decisions is not a part of it.

I return to my room and slam the door shut behind me. The sound reverberates through the quiet of the mansion, *but I don't care.*

I pace back and forth, reviewing Nikolai's orders and actions.

I shouldn't be questioning him.

It's a surefire way to get myself killed.

And then there's Alina.

I shouldn't have even gone there.

Fucking Nikolai's daughter is a dangerous game...

One that I can't afford to play.

But it's too late to change that now.

I shake my head, trying to rid myself of these thoughts. I walk over to my desk, reach into my pocket, and pull out my gun. I place it on the table and stare at it for a moment. I take a deep breath and pick up the gun again. The cold metal feels comforting in my hand as I check the chamber and ensure it's loaded.

As I set the gun down, there's a knock on my door. I know it's Stian before he even speaks. Without turning around, I say, "What do you want?"

Stian enters my room without waiting for an invitation, closing the door behind him. "What the fuck is wrong with you, Sullivan?"

"I have no idea what you are talking about."

"Bullshit," Stian says, walking over to stand before me. "I know you too well. You don't question Nikolai's orders. So, what's going on?"

I meet his gaze with a cold, steely stare. "Nothing."

Stian doesn't back down. He steps closer to me, his expression hardening. "Don't bullshit me, Kane. I can tell when something is off with you. Put your head back in the fucking game, or you will get yourself killed."

I stare at Stian.

He's right, of course.

I can't afford to let my guard down.

Not in this world.

Not with Nikolai as my boss.

Stian's eyes narrow, "Is it about Nikolai's daughter?"

I don't answer, *but my silence is answer enough.*

Stian curses under his breath, his fists clenching at his sides. "You're playing with fire, Sullivan," he warns, "Don't let your dick get in the way of the job."

"Alina is just work, Stian."

"Alina is not just any work. She's Nikolai's fucking daughter, and you do not want to fuck with her. Not in any way, shape, or form." he says in a menacing tone. "Just remember what's at stake here," he warns before turning and heading for the door.

I take a deep breath and turn to face Stian, "I don't need you to tell me how to do my job, Evensen."

"Then tell me, Kane," he says, "Are you catching feelings for the princess?"

I laugh coldly, the sound echoing through the room. "I don't catch feelings, Stian," I say emotionless, "That's not who I am."

Stian eyes me for a moment.

Finally, he nods. "Good," he says, turning to leave. "Because if you do, you know I won't be the one to take you down. But you will wish it was."

CHAPTER SEVEN

I wake up to the sound of my alarm blaring. The bright red numbers on the clock read 7 AM.

I stretch out in bed, feeling the familiar hardness between my legs. I slide my hand down my stomach, and my fingers trail down to my hardening length.

I don't have time for this. I need to be up before Alina.

My mind snaps to attention as I pull my hand away.

I throw the covers off me and get up, feeling the chill of the room hit my bare skin, and I quickly head to the bathroom.

As I splash cold water on my face and shake my head.

I grab a quick shower and dress in a black t-shirt and jeans, not bothering with anything fancy, standing in front of the mirror, pulling my hair back into a bun.

I leave my room and pass by Alina's door, which is still closed. I don't waste any time wondering if she's awake or not.

That's not my concern.

My job is to protect her, not worry about her morning routine.

I make my way downstairs to the living room, where the maids are setting breakfast down on the table. Nikolai is already there, dressed in a sharp suit and tie, ready to leave with Stian.

"Good morning, Mr. Sullivan," he greets me with a nod.

"Good morning, sir."

Nikolai turns to me, "Stian and I will leave for a few days, not sure how many. I need you to be all eyes on Alina."

I nod curtly, "Understood, sir."

Nikolai clasps a hand on my shoulder, his grip firm. "I know I can trust you, Kane," he says, "You are one of my best men for a reason."

I give him a slight nod.

I don't need his praise.

Nikolai gives me one last nod before he and Stian leave the room, leaving me to my duties.

I take a seat at the table, ignoring the maids as they fuss over me, pouring me coffee and offering me food.

I am finishing my breakfast when I hear the sound of footsteps coming down the stairs. I turn my head just in time to see Alina enter the room.

Despite the lack of sleep, *she looks stunning.*

Her hair is tousled, falling in loose waves around her shoulders. Her cheeks are slightly flushed, and her lips are plump and pink, *a sight that makes my body ache with longing.*

Her white silk dress hugs her curves in all the right places, accentuating her slender waist and toned legs. The dress has a low neckline, revealing just enough of her cleavage to make my pulse race.

Her skin is glowing, for fuck's sake.

Alina walks towards the table, and I follow her movements with my eyes.

Every step she takes.

Every sway of her hips...

It's like a magnet pulling me closer to her.

"Good morning," she says.

I nod in acknowledgment but don't say anything in response.

She sits across from me, and I continue eating my breakfast, keeping my eyes focused on the food.

"Cat got your tongue?" she raises an eyebrow.

I glance up at her briefly before returning my gaze to my plate. "No, just not in the mood for idle chatter."

"Well, I'm not exactly a morning person either, but I figured I should at least try to be civil."

I give her a slight nod, but my expression remains stoic.

I'm not here to be her friend or keep her company.

And I'm certainly not here to get distracted...

... again.

"Where's my father?"

"He left with Stian," I reply.

"Do you know where they went?"

"No," I reply, "It's not my concern."

She gives me a small nod. Her lips pressed into a thin line. "Of course, it's not. After all, all you do is follow his orders like a good puppy."

"And you? You are just as obedient to him, aren't you?" I take a sip of my coffee, studying her over the rim of my cup.

Alina's eyes narrow at my words, "I do what is necessary for my family."

I lean back in my chair, my gaze never leaving hers. "Just like I do what is necessary for myself."

She leans forward, "You are nothing but a pawn in my father's game."

I slam my hand on the table, causing the dishes to clatter. "Watch your mouth, Alina. You may be his daughter, but that doesn't mean I won't put you in your place."

"You wouldn't dare," she hisses.

"Oh, but I would," I reply, "Don't push me, princess."

I sit back in my chair, taking a deep breath to compose myself.

Alina clears her throat.

"Do you know how long he'll be away?"

I shake my head. "As I said before, I don't know. It could be a few days. It could be longer."

Alina smirks, her gaze locked on mine. "Well, lucky for us, I happen to enjoy spending time with you alone, Kane." She leans forward, "In fact, I can think of a few ways we could pass the time together." Her eyes flicker down my body, taking in my form with a heated look. "What do you say, Mr. Sullivan? Care to indulge in some... extracurricular activities?"

I lean back in my chair.

Unaffected by her words.

Sure...

Inside I imagine how good she would look underneath me, how her skin would feel against mine, and how her moans would sound in my ear. Her challenge has only fueled the desire that's been simmering within me, and I can't wait to unleash it on her.

I let my gaze wander down her curves, and my mind fills with images of her writhing beneath me, begging for more.

I push the thoughts aside...

I force myself to focus on the present.

Alina bites into a piece of freshly baked strawberry cake, and I watch as her lips close around the fork. "I'll be going out today," she says, breaking the silence between us.

I raise an eyebrow, waiting for her to continue explaining herself.

She takes another bite of cake, savoring the taste before speaking again. "I have some shopping to do, so I'll be away from home for a while."

"You are not going anywhere without me."

Alina gives me a mischievous grin, setting her fork down on the plate. "Actually, I meant to say that we are going shopping," she corrects, her eyes sparkling with amusement.

"Fine. But you're not leaving my sight," I warn her.

She shrugs, reaching for her coffee cup. "As you wish, Kane."

CHAPTER EIGHT

We've been walking around the stores for what feels like hours, and Alina has been buying everything she sees.

Clothes...

Shoes...

Jewelry...

You name it. She's got it.

Finally, Alina spots a store with underwear and lingerie, and she excitedly runs inside, making me follow her. I keep my expression neutral as I glance at the lacy and barely-there pieces.

Alina takes her time browsing through the racks, holding up different pieces of lingerie to her body and admiring herself in the mirror. She picks out a few pieces and disappears into a fitting room.

"I can't lose you from my sight," I follow her.

She turns to me, "Then you'll have to follow me in here," she says with a grin before disappearing behind the curtain.

Fantastic...

I hesitate for a moment.

Is it really necessary?

Of course, it isn't...

But then I hear the sound of fabric rustling...

And my resolve crumbles.

I follow her into the small changing area, my eyes are immediately drawn to her as she strips off her dress.

The sight of her in just her bra and panties makes my mouth go dry.

She's gorgeous...

And the way she moves is like a siren's call.

I can feel myself growing hard just looking at her.

No...

Keep your fucking distance, Kane.

"What do you think?" she asks, turning around to show me her back.

"It's..." My voice trails off as I take in the sight of her toned back and shapely curves.

I can't take my eyes off of her as she turns around, her back exposed and her curves accentuated by the lacy fabric. I can see the outline of her nipples through the material, making my mouth water and my cock throb with need.

"It's fine," I say shortly, not wanting to give away how much she's affecting me.

She frowns, sensing my lack of enthusiasm. "Just fine?"

"It's not really my area of expertise," I say dismissively.

But the truth is...

I want her in every way possible.

I shouldn't, but I do.

And seeing her in such revealing lingerie makes it nearly impossible to resist her.

I reach for the curtain and feel a hand on my arm, pulling me back. Alina is standing in front of me, her eyes sparkling.

"Let me show you what I got," she says, and before I can protest, she's slipping out of her lingerie and into another set.

I watch her, *transfixed*, as she moves with fluid grace.

Each piece she puts on is more daring than the last, and my mind races with all the things I want to do to her.

"What do you think now?" she asks, twirling around to show me every angle.

"It's...nice."

"You're not even looking," she complains.

I force myself to meet her gaze. "I'm looking," I say, my voice low. "But we should get going."

I turn to leave, but once again, she grabs my arm, pulling me back. "One more thing," she says, holding up a particularly daring piece of lingerie. "I want to try this on."

I can feel my control slipping away, but I force myself to stay detached. "Fine."

Alina disappears behind the curtain once more.

When she emerges, my eyes widen at the sight of her in the lacy two-piece lingerie. The panties hug her curves in all the right places, showing off the smooth skin of her pussy beneath, and the bra with heart shapes around the nipples leaves nothing to the imagination making me clench my fists to keep from reaching out and touching her.

Alina pulls me inside the curtain, and my heart races.

Before I can say anything, she turns to me and says, "Remember, Kane, you are my bodyguard. You need to be as close to me as possible."

She takes my hands and places them over her boobs. The lacey fabric is so thin I can feel the softness of her skin beneath it, and my thumbs brush over her uncovered nipples, making her groan and lick her lips.

I keep forgetting that I'm supposed to be detached...

I'm supposed to be professional.

All I can think about is how badly I want to fuck her...

I want to take her right here and now.

I take a step back, pull my hands away from her body, and clear my throat. "That's enough, Alina," I say, trying to hide the desire still coursing through my veins. "We should go. We have a long day ahead of us."

I watch Alina as she reaches for my length, her fingers brushing against the growing bulge in my pants. "It doesn't look like it's enough," she says, a mischievous glint in her eye. "Your body says otherwise."

I step closer to her.

My gaze locks onto hers.

I feel the heat between us.

My body is responding to her touch.

I grab her ass hard, pulling her against my body and biting her bottom lip before slapping her butt cheek. "You are a horny princess," I tell her, letting her go. "And you need to be taught a few things."

Alina looks up at me, her eyes full of lust, "Maybe you should teach me then," she says, a smile playing on her lips. She turns around, presenting her body to me. "I want you to show me everything."

I can't control myself anymore...

Not when I see her standing there in nothing but her lacey lingerie.

My eyes roam over her body, taking in every curve and every inch of smooth skin. "You have no idea what you're asking for."

She turns back to face me, "Try me," she says, stepping closer and pressing her body against mine.

I undo my belt slowly *and watch as Alina's eyes widen*.

I wrap it around her wrists, pulling her hands up and behind her back.

She gasps as I turn her around, pressing her back against my chest. I run my hand over her body, feeling the silkiness of the lingerie against my fingers.

I unbutton my jeans and slide them down, revealing my boxers. I push Alina's shoulders down, making her kneel in front of me. My heart pounds in my chest as I step out of my jeans and let them fall to the floor.

With one hand holding her chin, I use the other to open her mouth with my thumb.

I guide myself inside her mouth, feeling her warm, wet tongue wrap around me. I let out a low groan as I move in and out, setting a rhythm that has us both panting with need.

I watch her with half-closed eyes as she sucks me deeper into her mouth, her tongue swirling around the head of my cock.

I groan.

My hand tightens in her hair as I guide her movements.

She takes me in deep, gagging slightly but never backing away, the sight of her submitting to me sending me over the edge. With one last thrust, I come in her mouth, my hips jerking involuntarily.

"Swallow, princess."

She looks at me, and I repeat.

"Swallow it." I see her smile and continue, "If you don't, this will be a mess. And we don't do messes in public, do we now?"

She does as she is told and pulls away.

I can see the satisfaction on her face.

The thrill of pleasing me clear in her eyes.

I lift her up, pressing her against the wall and kissing her deeply.

My hands wander over her body, tracing the curves of her breasts and hips as she moans against my lips.

I release her lips, trailing kisses down her neck, nipping and licking at the sensitive skin. Alina's breathing is heavy and ragged.

She's eager for more...

... and so am I.

But I have to stop this before I do something I regret.

With a flick of my wrist, I untie the belt from her hands, letting it fall to the floor. I lift her leg, wrapping it around my waist as I press her harder against the wall.

Our bodies are pressed so close together that it's hard to tell where one ends and the other begins.

"Kane," she gasps, her fingers digging into my back. "I need you."

I smile against her neck, "But you see, princess," I say, pulling away from her, "I never said I would give you what you need."

"What do you mean? You're leaving me like this?" she asks, gesturing to her disheveled appearance.

I nod, pulling my shirt back on and pants up. "You can finish getting dressed so we can go home," I glance at my watch. "It's already late."

Alina gives me a smirk and licks her lips, "You think you've taught me all you can, Kane?" she says, running her fingers through her tousled hair. "I think there's more I can learn from you."

I raise an eyebrow at her challenge, "Dress up and let's go home."

I pull the curtain aside and step out, leaving her alone inside.

CHAPTER NINE

I step into the gym, taking in the spaciousness of the room. The Moskal mansion is a grand estate, and it's no surprise that they have their own gym. It saves me the trouble of leaving the house to train.

Plus, being inside means I don't have to be on top of Alina all the time, thanks to the guards outside the house.

My job is to know where she is...

But it doesn't mean I must watch her every second of the day when we are both inside.

I head to the cardio machine, starting my warm-up. The rhythmic pounding of my feet on the treadmill matches the thoughts running through my mind.

I grew up on the streets where violence and crime were a way of life. My parents were murdered, and Klara and I were lucky to escape with our lives, but we were separated soon after.

I ended up on the streets.

I met people who taught me how to fight and stand up for myself.

It was a brutal life...

... but it was all I knew.

One day, I met Stian.

Stian's story is different from mine.

He was already a member of the Moskal clan long before I came into the picture. He had a way out of his own struggles, and it was through them.

The day Stian approached me on the streets, I was in a fight, *as usual*. It was strange when he showed up and offered me money to fight with him, but I needed the cash, so I accepted it.

We battled it out.

Neither of us could take the other down.

Afterward, Stian approached me again and told me he had a place where I belonged.

It was perfect timing.

I was tired of living on the streets, always looking over my shoulder, and fighting to survive.

Stian took me to Nikolai.

The rest is history.

I'll never forget how Nikolai looked at me like he could see all the pain and hunger in my past.

He offered me a way out, a way to build a new life.

I took it, knowing that I could never go back to the life I had before.

I switch to the boxing area, going through a series of exercises that work on everything from my footwork to my reflexes.

In my world, weakness is not an option.

You either stay on top or get crushed underfoot.

I hit the punching bag with force, relishing the sting of impact on my knuckles.

When I started working for Nikolai, all my jobs were dirty.

I was hired to kill without reason or explanation.

It was a means to an end.

It was a paycheck to keep me going in a life where money was scarce.

But being a bodyguard for Alina is different.

It's the first time Nikolai doesn't hire me just to torture or shoot someone.

For once, I'm on the inside, *playing a bigger game.*

I pause to catch my breath, wiping the sweat from my brow.

I'm loyal to Nikolai.

But I'm not a fool.

I know I'm expendable in his eyes. But as long as I'm useful to him, I'll keep doing what I do best: *protecting Alina and doing whatever it takes to stay on top.*

I catch a glimpse of Alina out of the corner of my eye, leaning against the door frame.

She looks too polished and perfect to be in this place. I know I must look like a hot mess right now, my hair a wild mess and sweat pouring down my face. *I don't care.*

"What did the sandbox do to deserve that?" she asks, nodding towards the bag I just punched.

I don't have the energy to play along with her little games. "This isn't the time for your games," I turn away from her and focus on the bag before me.

Alina doesn't flinch at my cold response.

Instead, she straightens up and walks towards me. "I'm not playing any games. I just want to talk."

"Get a psychologist. I've heard they are amazing at listening when people talk to them."

"Wow... he knows how to make a joke."

"It was not a joke," I tell her.

I stop mid-punch and turn to face her, wiping the sweat off my forehead with the back of my hand.

"You never want just to talk, Alina. What do you want?"

I continue to hit the punching bag, and Alina walks over to one of the machines sitting down. She crosses her legs, puts her hands on her knee, and tilts her head slightly.

"Do you want to know why I wasn't affected by how you and Stian tortured that guy from the ball?" she asks, calm and collected.

I stop my punching and turn to face her. "Nope. I don't care."

Yes, I do.

"I think you do," she says, eyes boring into mine. "I saw how you looked at me when you realized I didn't flinch. You think I'm some fragile little thing who can't handle the brutality of this world. But I'm not. And you're not as flat-faced as you think you are."

"Again, Alina... you don't know me. How many times do I have to repeat the same thing?"

"I know enough," her eyes never leave mine. "I know it wasn't your choice to bring me along last night. And I know I would have been safe at home, surrounded by my father's best men, just like before you came into the picture."

"And what makes you so sure of that?"

"Because my father used to make me go with Stian on dirty work," she tells me. "He wants me to see the world's reality, to know how dark it is. It started happening after my mother was killed, so I was only a teenager when I started watching people getting tortured and murdered. As his successor, he ensures I'm inside and not just existing. He wants me to be ready for whatever the future holds."

I can feel the weight of her words settling in my chest.

I had an idea that Alina's life wasn't all sunshine and rainbows, but hearing it out loud makes it real in a way that I wasn't prepared for.

Alina raises an eyebrow. "You weren't expecting that, were you?"

"I'm not here to expect anything from anyone," I resume my punching.

Alina sighs and shakes her head. "I'm sick of your attitude like you are untouchable and nothing can move you."

I pause my workout and walk over to her. "It's not an attitude, Alina. It's the truth. I truly couldn't care less," I say, looking her straight in the eye.

"I know you're lying to yourself, Kane. You are not as cold as you pretend to be."

"Is there anything else you want to say?" I ask, and my tone indicates the conversation is over.

Alina rises to her feet, getting closer to me. "No one comes to work for my father because their life is easy. And I saw you around before this whole bodyguard thing. I know you worked for my father long before this."

"It's none of your business," I reply, turning away from her and walking towards the door.

"Do you want to know how my mom died?" she calls out after me.

I stop in my tracks but still don't turn to face her. "No. It's not my place to know that."

"Because my mother was being unfaithful to my father," Alina says, "She died because she was a Moskal, yes, but she didn't die at the hands of the Moskal's enemies. She died at the hands of her own husband."

I don't say anything.

I can't show any emotion.

After a few moments of silence, I finally turn to her. "Are you done?"

Alina shakes her head, and I leave the room without looking back.

•

As I head back to my room, Alina's words keep replaying. She opened up more than she should have, and now I know things I wasn't supposed to. I feel like an intruder in their family's personal affairs.

It's not my place to meddle in their business.

My duty is to protect Alina and make sure she's safe.

Not to get involved in their drama.

However, the fact that Nikolai killed his wife...

If he was capable of taking down his own spouse...

He might do the same to his daughter.

But I can't let it affect how I do my job.

I'm here to serve Nikolai, not Alina.

My loyalty lies with him.

CHAPTER TEN

I lie on my bed, staring at the ceiling, trying to clear my mind. It's been a long day, and I need rest.

I close my eyes.

I hear gunshots in the distance.

What's happening?

My eyes shoot open, and I jump out of bed, adrenaline coursing through my veins.

I rush to the window and peek outside, straining my eyes to see through the darkness. I hear sounds of glass breaking and more gunshots coming from the direction of the guards' post, but there's also another set of shots.

I quickly grab my two guns and stuff them in my trousers along with a knife before leaving my room, keeping low and moving quietly down the hallway toward Alina's room.

As I pass by the windows, I can see shadows moving outside and the sound of my footsteps echoing through the halls.

I reach Alina's room and burst through the door without knocking. She's standing near the window, looking out, and she jumps at the sound of the door slamming open.

"Are you crazy?" I ask, pulling her away from the window. "You'll catch a bullet in your head like that."

67

I quickly turn off all the room lights, ensuring we are not visible from the outside. "What's going on?" Alina asks.

"I don't know," I reply, "But most likely, they are here for you."

Alina's eyes widen as she looks up at me. "Do you have a gun?"

I hesitate for a moment.

Should I give her a gun?

Does she know how to use one?

But then I remember who she is.

I remember the family she comes from.

She most likely knows how to use a gun.

"I obviously do," I say, taking out one of my guns and handing it to her. "But only use it if it's absolutely necessary. And try not to shoot yourself in the process, please."

Alina takes the gun and checks the safety.

Yep, she does.

"Did you think I didn't know how to use one?" she asks.

I nod, "Being part of a family like yours... I guess it's a given."

We stand there in silence for a moment, listening to the sounds of chaos outside.

"What do we do now?" she asks.

I take a deep breath, "We wait. And we stay low until we know what's going on. We can't risk going out there blindly."

We wait in the hallway, and the sounds outside grow louder. Suddenly, the silence is broken by a loud crack as the house's front door is forced open. I quickly push Alina behind me, gesturing for her not to make a sound with my finger on my lips.

I crouch down on the top of the stairs and peek down into the darkness of the house. I can see the door open and two men getting inside, guns in their hands. They move quickly and quietly, their eyes scanning the room for movement.

I tighten my grip on my gun.

I'm ready to defend us if necessary.

Alina is pressed against me, her breathing shallow and rapid.

The men continue to move around the house, their footsteps echoing through the halls.

My heart is pounding, and there's sweat on my forehead.

I hear one of the men walking up the stairs, and I quickly put my gun back into my trousers and take out my combat knife from my pocket, holding it ready to take the man down without drawing any attention.

My eyes remain focused on the figure moving up the stairs, my mind calculating each step and movement he makes.

The man reaches the top of the stairs, and without making a sound, I rise from my crouched position, my movements graceful and fluid. I approach him from behind, my body pressing against his as I retrieve his gun with one hand, feeling the cool metal against my skin. With my other hand, I hold his body in place, ensuring that he remains silent and unable to move.

As I slide the sharp edge of my knife across the man's neck, his body weight begins to fall. With a quick reflex, I catch his body in my arms, and my muscles tense as I try to prevent any sound from escaping.

Any noise could alert the other man to our presence and put us in danger.

I wipe the blood from my combat knife on his shirt, the metallic smell filling my nostrils.

I turn to look at Alina, ensuring she's still with me.

She's approaching the body.

Searching for something.

I feel confused before she pulls a knife from the guy's body, giving me a proud smile. I shake my head and gesture that we need to move.

I stand up with my gun in my hand and hear the sound of footsteps approaching.

I immediately freeze.

My senses are on high alert.

I feel the adrenaline coursing through my veins as a man comes into view, his gun pointed in my direction.

Without hesitation, I push Alina down to the ground, out of the line of fire.

A gunshot rings in my ears...

... but I'm not hit.

The man is too far away to hit me.

I quickly take out my gun and shoot the guy in the leg, making him wince in pain. Before he can even make another sound, I hit him in the head, *ending his life.*

I turn to Alina and see her sitting on the ground, staring at me. "Shit," she mutters under her breath.

"Shhh," I tell her, "There are more where those two came from. The gunshot probably alerted them of where we are."

We move down the stairs, careful not to make any noise. We reach the bottom and hear voices from the room at the end of the hallway. I motion for Alina to stay put and silently approach the door.

Peeking inside, I see two more men.

Their backs are turned to me.

I take a deep breath, preparing myself for what needs to be done.

I burst into the room, my gun ready, and shoot them both before they even have a chance to react.

As I scan the area, I notice that the floor is clear.

Satisfied that there are no more threats, I turn my attention to the window. I step closer to it, trying to understand better what's happening outside.

A searing pain shoots through my arm, and I stumble back, clutching it tightly. I look up and see a figure holding a smoking gun in the distance. I take a deep breath, trying to focus and pull the trigger, but my aim is off, and the guy escapes unscathed.

I've been shot.

Just as I'm about to try again, I hear a loud bang from behind me. I spin around, my gun raised, and see the guy collapsing on the floor, lifeless. It takes me a moment to realize what's happened, but when I do, I see Alina standing there, her gun still smoking.

"Nice shot," I say, giving her a half-smile.

She rushes to me, "Are you okay?"

"I'll live," I say, gritting my teeth through the pain. "We need to ensure there aren't any more of them out there."

As if on cue, Nikolai's men come into view, their guns ready. One of them approaches us. "Everything's under control now," he says. "Go inside."

I grip my injured arm tightly, the pain radiating like a hot poker. Blood seeps through my fingers, staining my shirt a deep crimson.

I try to focus on Alina's face.

But my vision is starting to blur around the edges.

I'm finding it harder and harder to hear her words clearly.

I feel myself zoning out, losing consciousness as the weakness consumes me. I fight against it, knowing that we are not safe yet. I grab Alina's arm and stumble toward the stairs, each step feeling like a monumental effort.

We climb the stairs, and my energy drains away. My body grows weaker with each passing moment.

I finally collapse on the floor of Alina's room, feeling the darkness closing in around me.

Before I lose consciousness, *I feel Alina's touch.*

Her hand on my arm.

Her voice calling out to me.

"Kane, are you okay? Kane!"

I can barely hear her over the pounding in my head and the rushing sound in my ears.

CHAPTER ELEVEN

I start to feel consciousness returning to me

My body is heavy.

My arm is throbbing with pain.

I hear a distant voice calling my name and feel a gentle touch on my face.

It's Alina.

I try to open my eyes, but it's a struggle.

Finally, I manage to pry them open and see Alina's concerned face hovering over me. I groan, trying to sit up.

"Kane, you need to lay still," Alina says, trying to push me back down. "Your arm is badly hurt. You are losing too much blood."

I look around the room, realizing we are in her bedroom and the door is closed.

I need to do something.

I need to call Stian.

I reach for my phone, but my arm protests with sharp, shooting pains. Alina notices my struggle and touches my arm gently, "Kane, what are you doing? We need to take care of your arm first."

I don't answer.

I wait for Stian to pick up the phone.

After what feels like an eternity, he finally picks up.

"Stian, the house was under attack."

"How many?" Stian asks immediately.

"We took out five guys. They killed the guards outside to get in, but more of Nikolai's men are already here. I'm injured. I'm with Alina in her room."

There's a moment of silence on the other end of the line.

"I'm on my way. Stay put and keep low. Don't do anything stupid, Sullivan."

I hang up and look over at Alina. "What's happening?" she asks.

"Stian is on his way."

As I speak, Alina jumps into action, running to the bathroom in her room and returning with a first aid kit.

"Is managing guns not enough for you?" I joke, trying to distract myself from the pain.

She gives me a small smile as she starts to clean the wound.

What am I feeling?

I'm not sure what it is...

... but I know I shouldn't be feeling it.

She pulls up my t-shirt sleeve and applies physiological serum to the wound, washing it and making me wince.

"It's going to hurt," she warns as she puts a bandage on and applies pressure to control the bleeding. "I can't take the bullet out, but at least we can control the bleeding."

I nod, trying to focus on her words instead of the pain. "Thank you."

Alina stops and looks at me momentarily as if she wasn't expecting me to thank her. "Why are you thanking me?"

I look back at her and meet her gaze. "You saved my life."
Alina nods and looks back at my wound without a word.

•

I hear the sound of a car pulling up outside the mansion.
Stian is finally here.
Alina quickly puts the first aid kit away and helps me to sit up. I hear footsteps coming closer to the room.
He enters the room and looks at me, then at Alina.
I can tell he's assessing the situation.
He nods at Alina before turning his attention back to me. "Let me look at that wound," he says, coming closer and removing the bandage.
Alina moves away as Stian inspects my injury.
"It's not too deep, but we need to get that bullet out of there," he says. "I already called for people to come and take care of it. They'll be here soon."
I nod, knowing that Stian wouldn't leave anything to chance. He pulls me away from Alina's room, closing the door behind us. We walk a few steps down the hallway before he turns to face me.
"Nikolai couldn't come with me, but he wanted me to make sure that Alina is safe," Stian says.
I nod, "She's safe."
Stian's eyes dart toward Alina's room before he turns back to me. "Nikolai has given me orders to take you off the job if you are too injured to protect Alina."
My jaw clenches at the thought. "I'm not too injured," I say, "I can still do my job."

Stian's gaze bores into mine, "Kane, if something happens to Alina because you are not fit enough to protect her, Nikolai will have both our head."

I take a step closer to Stian. "I won't let anything happen to her."

Stian shakes his head and narrows his eyes, "I hope you're right," he says, "But I'll be watching you, Sullivan. Don't make me regret this."

I meet his gaze, unflinching. "You won't. I'll protect her with my life if I have to."

Stian's phone rings, and he picks it up without taking his eyes off me.

"Mr. Moskal," he says, his tone respectful.

My heart sinks.

He keeps his voice low. "Alina is safe. Kane's injury is not too bad. He can keep on protecting her."

He listens for a moment before responding.

"Yes, sir. Understood."

Stian hangs up and turns to me. "Remember, Sullivan. One wrong move, and we are all dead."

●

Stian has already left the house, leaving behind the reassurance that more of Nikolai's men were guarding the perimeter of the house.

Alina enters my room as I lie in bed.

I stay quiet, observing her movements.

She sits on the bed beside me and starts speaking, "How is that?" looking at my arm.

"They removed the bullet and took care of the wound. Everything's fine now."

She glances around the room before saying, "My father's people cleaned up the mess caused by the break-in. It's one of the perks of being part of the Moskal family, I guess. We have the power to control everything and everyone."

She starts lying down next to me.

"What are you doing?" I ask.

"I don't want to be alone in my room," she replies, putting her head on my chest.

I don't say anything.

I just let her be for a moment.

"Alina," I say finally, breaking the silence. "I don't think this is such a great idea."

"Why not?" she asks, looking up at me with those big agate eyes.

"You know the answer to that question."

"Everyone's gone now," she says softly. "And I really don't feel like being alone."

Her warm breath is on my neck.

I turn my head to look at her.

Her lips are so close to mine.

I reach up and brush my hand against her cheek, pulling her closer to me. Our lips meet in a soft, tentative kiss, but it quickly turns into something more.

Alina's hands run over my chest, and I feel the heat between us growing with every passing second.

I don't try to push her away.

I don't try to stop her.

Instead, I find myself engaging in the kiss.

It's like she's giving me life again, breathing air into my lungs that I didn't even know I needed.

We kiss, and I forget about everything else.

I forget about the bullet wound in my arm.

I forget about the men guarding the house.

I can only focus on Alina...

On how she's making me feel right now.

Her lips part as she deepens the kiss, her hands tangling in my hair. My body responds instinctively, my hands finding their way to her waist.

She breaks the kiss and looks down at me. I don't say anything, just reaching up to brush a strand of hair from her face.

She takes the lead, shifting her weight and sitting on my lap. She leans in for another kiss, her body pressing against mine as she wraps her arms around my neck.

I wince in pain as the throbbing ache in my wound intensifies.

"Are you okay?" she asks, reaching for my wound.

I nod, gritting my teeth. "I'm fine."

Alina doesn't look convinced, *but she doesn't push it.*

She leans in and presses her lips against mine once more. I respond with hunger, kissing her fiercely as my hands roam her. She moans softly into my mouth, and I let out a low growl as I grind against her hips.

She breaks the kiss and slides her hands down my chest.

Her fingers trace the contours of my muscles.

She leans in and nips at my earlobe, "You are so tense," she murmurs, "Let me help you relax."

Without warning, she grinds her hips against mine again, and my hands wander down her back, grasping her ass and pulling her closer.

I flip us over, positioning myself on top of her.

I lift my shirt over my head, tossing it aside as I lower my head so my lips trail down her neck as I nip and suck at her skin.

Alina gasps and arches into me, her hands running through my hair. I slide my hand down her stomach, dipping lower and lower until I reach her panties, pulling her dress slightly up. I slide my fingers underneath, feeling the wetness between her thighs.

She moans as I tease her, circling her clit with my thumb. I slide a finger inside her, and she writhes beneath me, her body begging for more.

I move my mouth back up to hers, our lips meeting in a fiery kiss as I slide another finger inside her. She rocks her hips against my hand, and I increase the pressure, feeling her body trembling beneath me.

I take my fingers away from her and bring them to my lips, tasting her sweet arousal. Alina watches me with a hungry look, and I can feel my desire growing by the second.

She retakes the lead, pushing me back onto the bed and straddling me.

Her hands roam my chest.

Her mouth finds mine again.

And she kisses me fiercely as she grinds against my hardening length.

"I want you, Kane," she whispers.

Shit, princess.

I nod.

... I am unable to resist her any longer.

I undo my pants, freeing my aching cock, and she takes me in her hand, stroking me slowly as she looks into my eyes.

I growl with pleasure, my hands gripping her hips as I guide her onto me.

She sinks onto me with a gasp.

Her eyes close as she takes me in.

We move together, our bodies entwined, and I feel the heat building between us.

Alina's movements are slow at first, but she picks up the pace, her body moving perfectly with mine. She moans loudly, her head thrown back in pleasure, and I can feel myself getting close.

I take her nipples between my fingers, pinching them lightly as I feel the familiar tension building in my body.

Alina's movements become more urgent.

I know she's close.

I flip us over so I'm on top, my hands gripping her thighs as I pound into her relentlessly.

Her moans become louder.

Her nails dig into my back.

I can feel myself getting closer and closer.

I feel her walls tightening around me, so I quicken my pace, thrusting harder into her.

She arches her back.

Her hands grip the sheets as she cries out...

... and her orgasm washes over her in waves.

I continue to move inside her, the sensation pushing me over the edge. I let out a guttural groan as I come undone, my body shaking with pleasure.

With one final thrust, I explode inside her, and she cries out my name.

CHAPTER TWELVE

I jolt awake.

My heart races as if I'm in the middle of a hit.

But it's just Alina, restless in her sleep.

She's still clinging to me, her head resting on my chest, her breath hot against my skin.

I glance down at her, taking in her chest's slow rise and fall.

She used to be just a job.

Nothing more.

But now...

I can't deny there's something else to it.

I find myself worrying about her safety, not just because of what Nikolai would do to me if she got hurt, but because I don't want anything bad to happen to her.

I slide out of bed, careful not to jostle her. I settle her onto the mattress, tucking the blankets around her.

She mumbles something in her sleep but stays put.

I head to the kitchen, still feeling her weight in my arms, and pour myself a glass of water and grab a couple of painkillers.

I freeze when I see the lights outside.

Stian's car.

Shit.

I wasn't expecting them to be home tonight.

If Nikolai finds Alina in my bed, I'm screwed.

The door creaks open and in walk Stian and Nikolai. My heart races, and I force myself to appear calm, *praying* they don't head upstairs.

"How's the injury, Mr. Sullivan?" Nikolai questions, striding towards me and looming over me like a predator.

"It's nothing serious," I say, my eyes flicking to Stian before returning to Nikolai's steely gaze.

"Stian told me it was minor," He claps a hand on my shoulder, and I bite back a groan of pain, refusing to show weakness. "You better be in top shape, Kane. We have work to do."

I grit my teeth *and nod again*, hoping they won't notice the beads of sweat forming on my forehead.

Nikolai walks away, heading towards his office.

I let out a breath and watch as Stian looks at me momentarily before following Nikolai.

I quickly make my way up the stairs and enter my room. "Alina," I whisper as I gently shake her shoulder. "Your father is home. You must go to your room before he finds you sleeping in my bed."

She stirs awake, confusion written all over her face. "What?"

"Just go to your room, please." I repeat, a little more urgently this time.

She nods and gets up, standing in front of me for a moment. And then, without warning, she cups my face with her hand and gives me a soft kiss on the lips.

It's brief.

But it's enough to make me forget about everything else for a second.

And just like that, she's gone.

•

I'm pulled from my slumber by the sound of Stian's voice. "Sullivan, wake up," he says sharply. "It's past your waking time, and Nikolai wants to talk to you in his office."

I grunt, feeling the ache in my arm from the bullet wound. Stian's right.

I've been sloppy.

And Nikolai doesn't tolerate sloppiness.

I swing out of bed and stand, gritting my teeth against the pain.

Stian continues, "You need to get your shit together, Kane. Nikolai won't be happy if you keep slipping up like this."

I don't need Stian to tell me that. I know it.

"The alarm didn't go off," I say, pulling on a black t-shirt and trousers. I wince as I lift my arm to tie my hair back in a bun. "What did Nikolai say he wanted to talk about?"

Stian shakes his head. "He didn't say, but you know how he is. Don't keep him waiting."

I nod, already heading towards the door. "I won't."

I know I need to be careful.

Nikolai doesn't give second chances.

And I can't afford to mess up.

I leave my room and follow Stian to Nikolai's office. I feel the pain from the gunshot wound in my arm as I move, but I don't show it. Stian doesn't say a word, and I follow him into the office.

Nikolai is sitting behind his desk, smoking a Cuban cigar. He motions for me to sit in front of him and for Stian to close the door. I take a minute before sitting down, waiting for Nikolai to speak.

"How's your arm?" he asks, blowing smoke in my direction.

"It's fine."

Nikolai chuckles. "Perfect. Because I have a job for you, I need you to be in top shape."

I don't say anything, waiting for him to continue.

"It's a simple job. I need you to retrieve something for me. And I was hoping you could do it discreetly. No sloppiness allowed," he says, staring at me.

Retrieve something?

Did the men from yesterday manage to take anything away before I got them?

"Understood." I nod, "What about Alina?"

Nikolai gives me a half smile. "Alina will stay home. You are not playing bodyguard today."

I nod again. "All right."

Nikolai leans forward, his eyes locked on mine. "This job is important, Kane. I need you to handle it with the utmost care."

"Consider it done."

Stian leaves the room, leaving me alone with Nikolai. I feel his eyes on me, assessing my readiness for the job. I don't flinch, waiting for him to give me more details.

"You will be going alone," he says, handing me a piece of paper with an address scrawled. "It's a black leather bag that you need to retrieve. And Kane, it must never be opened. My orders."

I nod, taking the paper from him. "Understood."

Nikolai leans back in his chair, taking a long drag from his cigar. "This is important, Kane. If anything goes wrong, you know the consequences."

Failure is not an option in this world.

"I won't let you down," I reply coldly.

Nikolai nods, dismissing me with a wave of his hand.

Stian is waiting outside the door, his arms crossed. "You know the drill, Sullivan," he says gruffly. "You go in, and you get out. No questions asked."

"Who will protect Alina while I'm gone?"

Stian sighs, his eyes closing briefly. "Sullivan, we've been through this."

"I just want to do my job," I reply evenly. "And my job is protecting Alina."

Stian's expression hardens. "Your job is whatever Nikolai wants it to be, Sullivan. And today, it's not protecting Alina. So, keep your head in the game, or you won't be keeping a head at all."

"The house was attacked last night," I say, "And it could happen again. I won't be here to protect her."

Stian shakes his head, "Fuck. You got shot last night, Kane. How do you think you will protect Alina with your arm fucked up like that?"

I turn my face away.

"It's probably for the best," his tone final. "The house is more guarded than ever after the incident. Nothing is going to happen to Alina."

I turn to leave, then I pause and look back at the sound of his voice.

"Just be careful out there, Sullivan. We need you back in one piece."

I take a deep breath as I make my way up the stairs.

I need to get everything ready to leave.

I reach the top of the stairs, and Alina leaves her room, standing before me.

She smiles at me, but I can't return it. I nod and walk past her, hoping to avoid any conversation.

She calls out to me, stopping me in the hall.

Of course, she does.

"What's wrong, Kane?"

"I have a job to do," I reply curtly, not wanting to explain further.

"What kind of job?" she follows me.

I don't turn to face her as I respond, "One that you are not coming on."

"Is your job not to protect me?"

"My job is whatever your father wants it to be," I snap back.

"How long will you be gone?"

"I don't know," I tell her, "And it doesn't matter."

I can feel her eyes on my back as I walk into my room...

... but I don't turn around.

•

I grab my bag, filled with weapons, and go to the car.

As I close the trunk, I catch Alina's silhouette at the house's entrance, watching me.

She walks towards me.

Her hips sway with each step.

It's like a seductive dance that makes my pulse race.

"Are you coming back?"

I take my sunglasses off and put them on my shirt, looking around before answering. "I'm planning on it."

She reaches out to touch my arm. "Does it still hurt?"

"I'm all right," I reply, moving away from her.

She reaches for my hand and pulls me back, her gaze locked onto mine.

"Don't." I warn her, "You shouldn't be here. Your father has eyes everywhere. Seeing you so close to me like this is not good for either of us."

Alina ignores my warning and leans closer, her breath warm on my cheek. "I don't care about that," she whispers, her lips dangerously close to mine. "I just care about you."

I can feel my resolve slipping away as her words wash over me.

Part of me wants to give in to the temptation.

Forget everything else and be with her.

But I know better...

Especially when it comes to her.

"You have to go back inside," I tell her, pulling away from her grasp.

She pouts for a moment but then nods. "Just promise me you'll come back."

"I'll do my best," I reply before turning and getting into the car.

CHAPTER THIRTEEN

I park the car at the base of a hill and make my way up, careful not to make a sound.

I've been trained in stealth...

So, I put my skills to use as I navigate through the trees and rocks.

As I approach the building, my senses on high alert, I hear the sound of footsteps getting closer. I quickly take cover behind a nearby tree and wait. A group of armed men comes into view, their guns ready. I watch as they enter the building through the front door.

I wait a few minutes before making my way to the entrance. I peer inside and see the men gathered near a table.

I take a step back, formulating a plan.

I need to get closer without being seen.

I move toward the shadows, my back against the wall, and slowly approach the table. I see the black leather bag in the middle as I get closer.

Just as I'm about to grab the bag, one of the men spots me. "Hey, who's there?" he calls out, drawing the attention of the others.

I don't hesitate.

I grab the bag and run for it, dodging bullets.

I feel the adrenaline pumping through my veins, my heart pounding. I reach the door and burst into the open air, sprinting towards my car.

The bag is heavy, weighing down my arm with each step. I know that whatever is inside is valuable, and I must get it to safety as quickly as possible.

The men follow me, their footsteps pounding against the pavement. I reach my car and quickly unlock the trunk, shoving the bag inside. I grab my gun and turn, aiming it at the men as they emerge from the building. They pause for a moment, weighing their options as I make a run for it. One of the men lunges towards me, aiming his gun at my head. I quickly duck and spin around, swiftly kicking his abdomen. He falls to the ground, gasping for air.

Another man charges toward me, but I grab his arm and use his momentum to throw him over my shoulder, sending him crashing to the ground.

More men are closing in.

I take cover behind the car.

My arm is throbbing in pain.

I look down to check on the bullet wound on my upper arm. I grit my teeth and try to ignore the pain. The adrenaline still pumps through my veins, keeping me focused and alert.

I emerge from behind the car and charge toward the remaining men, firing my gun as I go. I grab one of them by the collar and punch his face, causing him to stumble backward.

Another man lunges at me with a knife, but he is careless enough to let me grab his wrist and twist it, causing him to drop it. I take the opportunity to disarm and knock him out with a quick blow to the head.

The last man standing tries to make a run for it.

But I won't let him escape.

I chase after him, and I finally catch up to him.

I tackle him to the ground as he struggles beneath me. I grab his gun and aim it at his head. I shoot him and return to the car as I hear more men coming.

I get into the driver's seat and start the car, revving the engine. As I pull away, I see the men regrouping.

I drive at breakneck speed, my heart still pounding and my arm hurting like shit. I glance in the rearview mirror, watching the men's cars come into view, closing in on me.

I sharply turn and slam on the brakes, causing their cars to skid past me. I jump out of the car, aiming my gun at the first man who emerges.

He fires...

And I dodge the bullet, rolling onto the ground.

I return fire, taking out two men before they can even react. I hear more footsteps coming from behind, and I spin around, firing at the next wave of attackers.

The gunshots echo through the air like a symphony.

I take cover behind a nearby car, reloading my gun as I catch my breath. I hear something approaching, and I aim, ready for whatever comes my way. But it's just a stray dog, barking and howling in the chaos.

I stand up, return to my car, and drive away.

I speed down the empty road and feel a sharp pain in my arm. I look down and see blood seeping through my shirt. "A simple mission, my ass..."

•

I keep driving for miles, dialing Stian's number repeatedly, but he doesn't answer.

Hours later, I arrive at the entrance of the mansion. The guards are all in position but look more alert than I've ever seen them. "What the fuck is happening here?"

I try not to use my injured arm as I make my way through the winding roads of the property. As I approach the main house, I see armed men gathered outside, their weapons ready.

I come to a stop and assess the situation.

Something has gone wrong.

I step out of the car and raise my hands. "Kane Sullivan."

The men hesitate for a moment before one of them, Fabian, steps forward.

"Follow me," he says, gesturing for me to come closer.

I follow him inside, my heart racing through the quiet halls. We finally reach Nikolai's office, and I see Stian's shirt covered in blood.

"What the hell happened?" I ask.

Before they can answer, I sprint upstairs, calling Alina's name as I go. But when I reach her room, it's a complete disaster.

Clothes are scattered all over the floor.

The drawers have been ripped out and emptied.

My panic rises as I realize it.

Alina is nowhere to be found.

I hurry back downstairs, past the guards, and towards Nikolai and Stian. "Where the fuck is Alina?"

Nikolai's face is grim when he speaks. "Someone took my daughter, Mr. Sullivan. They took her."

My heart sinks at his words.

•

I sit next to Stian as the medics patch up his wound. Nikolai is outside, talking to the guards and ensuring everyone is searching for Alina.

I turn to Stian, my voice low. "What happened while I was gone?"

Stian glances over at Nikolai to ensure he's out of earshot before he whispers back to me, "It was all of a sudden. There was nothing out of the ordinary, nothing suspicious. I was guarding the door outside Nikolai's office when two guys came out of nowhere and took me down. It was odd. They knew exactly where to go." He pauses, wincing in pain as the medics continue their work. "**They** didn't even try to enter Nikolai's office after they shot me."

Stian's story doesn't sit right with me.

If the attackers wanted to hurt Alina only to get to Nikolai, why would they go through the trouble of taking down Stian and not harming Nikolai in any way?

"I don't understand," I say to Stian. "If they wanted Nikolai, why go after Alina? He's right here."

"I don't know," he says with a shrug. "But after they shot me, they ran upstairs to Alina's room. I got up and tried to follow them, but another guy came out and knocked me unconscious. The last thing I remember is Alina screaming."

My stomach churns with a sickening feeling as I imagine Alina being taken, her screams echoing through the empty halls.

CHAPTER FOURTEEN

"Find my daughter, Kane. Find her before they hurt her. And bring her back to me unharmed."

I nod and make my way through the halls to her room.

I comb through the chaos, searching for clues that could lead me to Alina. My eyes dart around the room, looking for anything out of place.

"Shit," I mutter, "Maybe there's a lead somewhere. Where are you, princess?"

I pace back and forth in the room...

My mind is racing with possibilities.

If anyone lays a hand on Alina, I'll make them pay.

I won't hesitate to make them regret ever crossing me.

I'll break their bones one by one, making sure they suffer every excruciating moment. I'll beat them until they beg for mercy, but I won't stop there. I'll keep going until they are nothing but a bloody pulp at my feet.

I'll use every tool at my disposal.

Every weapon in my arsenal.

They'll wish they were dead when I'm done with them...

And they will be.

I leave Alina's room as I feel the fire burning inside me. I need to find those bastards who took her and make them pay.

I walk into Nikolai's office.

He is on the phone with Stian beside him. I don't bother to leave the room while he talks. Instead, I stand there with a blank expression on my face, waiting for him to finish.

When he finally hangs up, he turns to me and says, "Kane, just the man I wanted to see."

I wait for him to continue, my eyes locked onto his.

"I just spoke with Alina's captors," he says. "I know where she is and what they want. They want a life for a life. They want me to come alone and bring them some money, and myself, of course."

"And you are going to do it?"

Nikolai nods. "I have to. They have my daughter."

I step forward, "What do you need me to do?" knowing he won't just die there.

"I need you to make sure they don't try anything. I need you to make sure Alina and I come back alive."

Stian, who had been listening in, speaks up. "I'm coming with you."

Nikolai shakes his head. "No, you are not, Mr. Evenson. You are injured, and you need to recover. I can't risk losing more of my men."

"Mr. Moskal, I can handle it," Stian insists.

Nikolai's expression hardens. "I said no. You stay here. Kane will be the one coming with me."

I clear my throat, interjecting, "Mr. Moskal, what's the plan?"

Nikolai looks at me. "We're meeting them at an abandoned warehouse on the outskirts of town. I'll hand over the money, and they will give me Alina back. But I need you to be on high alert, Kane. These are dangerous people, and they won't think twice before taking us out. In fact, they plan to eliminate me, but they'll likely target both Alina and me."

I nod, my mind already racing with strategies and backup plans. "Understood."

Nikolai hands me a briefcase. "Inside is the money they want. It's a lot, but it's coming back with us after the job is done."

I take the briefcase and open it, seeing stacks of cash inside.

"When I surrender to the men waiting for me, I need you to go back and look for Alina. Get out of there with her safe and sound. Don't let anyone see you. We can't risk losing her again." Nikolai's face hardens. "And Kane, as soon as she is safe, I want you to take them out, one by one. I don't care what it takes. I want my daughter back, but I want them to pay for their actions. No one touches my daughter in any way and gets away with it."

My lips curl into a small, cold smile. "Consider it done."

•

I follow Nikolai's car on my own, ensuring we keep a safe distance. We park at different locations to avoid suspicion as we head toward the abandoned warehouse. Nikolai takes the briefcase filled with money, and I prepare myself with my gun and combat knife, ready to protect myself and find Alina.

As I watch Nikolai surrender to a man with a gun, I silently slip around the building, scanning every corner for any sign of Alina.

The emptiness of the warehouse echoes with every step I take, and I try to keep my movements as silent as possible to avoid detection.

The darkness makes it difficult to see, and I can barely make out the shapes before me.

I try to open the doors, *but they're all locked*.

My heart is pounding in my chest, and my palms are sweaty.

I move cautiously down a dimly lit hallway, my eyes scanning every corner for any sign of Alina.

Suddenly, a guard steps out of a doorway, blocking my path. I pull out my knife and take him out swiftly, silently.

My heart is racing with adrenaline.

I continue down the hallway, checking every room.

Still, there's no sign of Alina.

I continue searching, moving silently, and checking every nook and cranny, until I hear footsteps approaching. Quickly, I duck behind a stack of crates. I watch as the guard walks past me, scanning the area with his gun in hand.

As soon as he's out of sight, I follow him quietly, keeping my distance until he stops outside a door. I hear voices coming from inside. I silently take him out, then listen for any sounds that may lead me to her.

A soft whimper catches my attention, and I freeze, carefully trying to locate the source. I make my way toward the sound, my gun at the ready. As I approach, I see a figure huddled in the corner and quickly realize...

It's Alina.

I rush over to her, quickly checking to ensure she's not injured. She's tied up with tape on her mouth, but otherwise, she seems unharmed. I pull out my knife and cut the ropes, binding her hands.

"Shh, it's me," I whisper, trying to soothe her.

She looks up at me, her eyes wide.

I remove the tape from her mouth, and she starts to speak, but I quickly silence her with a finger to my lips.

"We need to get out of here quietly," I whisper. "Do you understand?"

She nods, and I quickly cut the ropes binding her ankles. I motion for her to follow me, and we start going back down the corridor. We move silently, keeping close to the walls and avoiding any guards.

As we approach a corner, I hear footsteps coming toward us. I quickly pull Alina into a nearby doorway, pressing her against the wall.

I take up a position next to her.

My gun ready to go.

The footsteps grow louder, and I hear the sound of voices. The group of men passes us by, completely unaware of our presence.

We wait a few moments, ensuring they are out of earshot, before continuing down the corridor.

We approach the exit, I motion for Alina to stay behind me, and the door opens.

Nikolai.

Nikolai's laughter echoes through the room as he steps forward, clapping his hands. Two men appear behind him, both pointing their guns at me. I keep my gun pointed at Nikolai, ready to fire at any moment if needed.

"Well done, Mr. Sullivan," Nikolai says. "If I didn't know better, I would say you were a good choice as my daughter's bodyguard."

Alina steps forward, trying to approach her father, but I quickly block her way with one arm, shaking my head in warning.

"What's happening?" Alina asks, clearly confused.

Nikolai continues to laugh. "I was testing Mr. Sullivan here. And he passed the test. Though, I'm unsure if that's good or bad in this situation."

Alina's eyes widen, "What test? What's going on?"

I keep my gun pointed at Nikolai as I answer her. "Seems like your kidnapping wasn't a simple kidnapping, Alina."

Nikolai's laughter dies down, replaced with a stern look. "Well, well. You are a smart guy, Kane. It's a shame you couldn't know your place."

"Was this whole mission even real, or was it just a ploy to gain time to abduct your daughter, Mr. Moskal?"

Nikolai tilts his head and smirks. "Oh, no, Mr. Sullivan. That bag belongs to me. I needed what's inside, but having you unwittingly get it for me while I planned the grand finale was helpful."

"You son of a bitch," I growl.

"We are leaving," Alina says firmly.

But Nikolai steps forward, his gun now in hand pointed at me. "I'm afraid you can't leave. Not yet, anyway. You see, I have some business to discuss with Kane."

Nikolai motions to his men, and one of them approaches Alina.

I try to stop him, "Keep your fucking hands away from her."
But before I can reach him, Nikolai has his gun against my
head, "Mr. Sullivan, if I were you, I wouldn't move much.
There's a chance I'll blow your brains out in a second."

The other man grabs my gun, and I feel a sinking feeling in
my gut, "Let her go!" I growl, my eyes locked on Alina as she
fights against the man who's trying to take her away.

Nikolai chuckles. "You are quite the fighter, Kane. But I'm
afraid you are outnumbered and outmatched here."

As they take Alina away, she screams and fights against
them, tears streaming down her face.

I try to go after her...

But before I know it...

... *everything is dark.*

CHAPTER FIFTEEN

I wake up with a groan.

My head is throbbing.

My arms are restrained behind my back.

I try to move, but the ropes are too tight.

I'm trapped in a chair.

As my eyes adjust to the dimly lit room, I see Nikolai sitting before me, puffing on a cigar. The smoke fills my nostrils, and I cough, struggling to breathe.

Nikolai chuckles and blows some smoke in my direction. "You know, Kane, I always thought you were smarter than this. Crossing me was not a good idea."

I don't reply, and Nikolai gets up, and before I can react, he punches me, hitting me in the mouth.

Blood fills my mouth, and I lick my lip, tasting the metallic tang. He laughs before throwing another punch, this time hitting me in the stomach.

"Not clever of you, Kane," he says, wiping his hand with a cloth. "Getting involved with my daughter was not clever of you."

I stay silent.

I know my words will only worsen things.

Nikolai gestures, and a man enters the room, holding Alina by the arm.

My heart sinks at the sight of her struggling to get free.

Nikolai tells the man to release her and dismisses him.

Alina runs to me, cupping my face and kissing me, "Oh my God, Kane!"

Nikolai shakes his head, clearly unimpressed. "Alina, you can't take a hint, can you?"

Alina walks over to her father, looking at him angrily. "Don't you dare touch him like that again."

Nikolai grabs her arm, twisting it. "You are my daughter, but remember, I have no problems taking a Moskal down," he says, throwing her to the floor.

I struggle against the ropes, trying to free myself...

But it's useless.

All I can do is watch Alina lie on the ground, *her face contorted in pain.*

Nikolai walks to her and moves her chin up, his eyes cold and unfeeling. "Now, you are going to learn what happens when you cross your Papa," he says, smiling at her and walking over to me.

Alina's tears stream down her face. "Please, Papa, don't hurt him."

Nikolai turns to her, "This is your fault, Alina," he says, his voice low and menacing. "You are just a little whore who doesn't know how to follow the rules. You brought this on yourself."

I try to speak up.

I try to defend Alina.

But I can't do it.

Nikolai stands in front of me and punches me again in the guts.

I double over in pain, *gasping for breath*.

"Stop it, please!" Alina cries out, crawling towards us on her hands and knees. "Stop hurting him. He didn't do anything wrong!"

"Did you think I wouldn't notice?" Nikolai asks.

I try to lift my head and say anything, *but the pain is too much*.

I feel the blood dripping down my face as I look at Alina, her makeup smudged from tears. I can see the fear in her eyes as Nikolai speaks to her. "You are just like your mother, child," he says, and Alina sobs uncontrollably. "You learned nothing from her death, did you?"

"Papa, please. I beg you. Don't kill him," Alina cries out, desperation in her voice.

Nikolai turns to her, crouching down and patting her on the head. "Oh, my princess. I am not killing him just yet... we have a long way to go until we get there."

He walks back towards me, leaving Alina on the floor.

As he turns his back to her, she tries to get closer to me, but he quickly grabs a hammer from the table beside me and points it at her, "You don't want to do that, Alina."

I flinch as Nikolai swings the hammer toward my knee, causing Alina to scream. Nikolai laughs aloud, stopping before hitting my bone, relishing in the terror he's causing.

This man is truly evil.

I look over at Alina, and my heart breaks at the sight of her.

She's so scared...

And I can't do anything to change that.

"I understand that you want to make a point, Nikolai, but she doesn't need to see this," I plead, my voice strained from the pain.

He raises an eyebrow and chuckles. "Oh, but that's the whole point, Kane. She needs to see what happens when people cross me," he says, walking over to the table and picking up a pair of pliers.

I try to brace myself as Nikolai grabs my finger with the pliers and begins to twist.

The pain is unbearable.

I scream in agony, my body writhing in the chair.

Alina covers her face with her hands, *sobbing uncontrollably.*

Nikolai looks at her and sneers. "Watch closely, my dear. This is what happens to those who betray me."

The door behind Nikolai suddenly opens, and a familiar voice speaks out, "Put your hands up where I can see them, Nikolai."

Alina jumps from the floor, sobbing, and runs to me, grabbing a knife from the table and cutting me loose. Stian has his gun pointed at Nikolai's head, and his *eyes locked on him.*

Nikolai raises his eyebrows, seemingly amused. "Well, well, well. It seems like traitors surround me."

Stian doesn't flinch as he unlocks the gun. "You've got people shooting me, you motherfucker."

Nikolai scoffs. "Come on, don't be such a drama queen, Evensen. It was only a scratch..."

Stian hits Nikolai in the head with his gun, making him fall unconscious on the floor.

I grunt in pain as Stian helps me up, and Alina retrieves her father's gun from him. "Shouldn't we tie him up somewhere?" Alina suggests.

Stian shakes his head, "We don't have time for that. Nikolai has eyes everywhere, and more of them are coming."

Alina holds the gun pointed at her father's body lying on the floor, and I speak out in pain, "Alina, don't." Alina sobs and sniffles, and I continue, "You will never be the same if you do that. Please, don't."

She retrieves the gun and walks with Stian and me out of the room.

I stumble as Stian helps me to keep myself straight on my feet, grunting in pain as my broken bones scream in protest. Alina supports me on the other side as we hobble towards the door.

My ribs ache with every breath.

"Come on, Kane," Stian encourages me, "We're almost there."

We make our way down the corridor, trying to move as quickly and quietly as possible. We hear the sound of footsteps and voices coming from somewhere nearby, and my heart races.

Finally, we make it outside.

Stian leads us toward his waiting car and helps me into the back seat, with Alina climbing next to me.

"Where are we going?" I ask.

"Somewhere safe," Stian replies, getting into the driver's seat.

I nod, wincing as the car starts moving.

Alina stays by my side, holding my hand tightly. The pain in my ribs is almost unbearable, and I try to take deep breaths to calm myself down.

"How did you find out about Nikolai's plan?" I ask Stian.

Stian glances at me through the rearview mirror before answering. "Nikolai doesn't worry about anyone, but back in the house, he was pretty insistent on keeping me home and away from getting Alina back. He would want all his men to get Alina back in a normal circumstance, so I noticed something was wrong."

I nod, trying to piece everything together in my head. "And the men that took Alina... they knew exactly what to do inside the house."

Stian nods. "Exactly. They knew where to go and not to hurt Nikolai. It was all too planned."

I shake my head, "I can't believe I was so blind."

Stian glances at me again. "You're not the only one, Kane. He had everyone fooled."

We drive in silence for a while before Stian speaks again. "We're almost there."

I open my eyes, looking out the window.

I don't recognize the place we are going to.

But at this point...

... *I don't care.*

CHAPTER SIXTEEN

Stian leads us into a room with a couch. I collapse onto it, groaning in pain. Alina sits beside me, and Stian kneels beside me, examining my injuries.

"This isn't good," he mutters, his eyes narrowing as he takes in the extent of my injuries.

"What are we going to do?" Alina's voice trembles.

Stian stands up and heads for the kitchen. "I have some medical supplies here," he calls back. "I'll get them."

As Stian rummages through a drawer, I look around the room, trying to distract myself from the pain.

The room is small and sparsely furnished, with only a few pieces of old furniture scattered around. I see a small table with a lamp, a bookshelf with some dusty volumes, and a fireplace with a few logs piled beside it.

It's not luxurious as the Moskal mansion.

But it's a relief to be somewhere safe.

Stian returns with the first aid kit, and I wince as he begins to clean and bandage my wounds.

"Where are we?" Alina asks, breaking the silence.

"This is my family's house. It's hidden in the woods," he explains. "I don't have any family to worry about, so the house is only mine. Nikolai doesn't even know about it. When I started working for him, I made sure he knew nothing about my origins."

"Thank you for bringing us here," Alina says quietly.

Stian nods, silence taking over the room again.

•

Stian went to the Moskal's to get us some clothes earlier. He just waltzed in and came back with the clothes, no problem. I have yet to learn how he did it without running into any of Nikolai's men, but he's always been fearless like that.

I try to push myself up from the bed to shower and change clothes, but my muscles scream in protest. Alina rushes over to me, placing a gentle hand on my back. "Let me help you," she says softly.

I don't protest as she helps me to my feet, supporting me as I hobble toward the bathroom. I lean heavily against the sink.

"Do you need any help?" Alina asks.

I shake my head at first, not wanting to show any more weakness than I already have. But as I struggle to lift my shirt over my head, the pain becomes too much to bear. "Actually... yeah. I could use some help."

Alina nods.

Her eyes are tender as she gently helps me remove my shirt, taking her time to be as gentle as possible as her fingers brush against my skin.

I glimpse myself in the mirror and wince at my bruised body. "Thank you," I say, looking at her image in the mirror.

I am silent as Alina turns on the water to warm up, admiring her beauty.

Her gaze meets mine, and she smiles softly.

I watch as she strips off her dirty dress, revealing her delicate lace white panties and perky, bare breasts. My breath catches in my throat as she turns to me and slowly removes my trousers and boxers.

I step into the shower and let the warm water wash over me, closing my eyes and letting out a sigh. Alina hands me a bar of soap, and I begin to lather up, feeling the stress melting away under her gentle touch.

She works her fingers through my hair, through the knots as the water cascades down my back.

The tension melts away with each stroke of her fingers.

My eyes flutter closed as she leans closer, "Let me take care of you," she whispers, barely above a murmur.

I turn to face her, the water falling over our bodies as we stand inches apart. She reaches for the shampoo, her fingers running through my hair again, massaging my scalp as she works the suds through my strands.

My hands find their way to her hips, pulling her closer to me. Her skin is soft and warm against mine,

With a soft sigh, she steps back and rinses the shampoo from my hair.

I watch as the water trails down her curves, feeling my desire for her grow stronger with each passing moment despite the bruises that still ache across my body.

As Alina works her way down my body, her hands glide over my skin, soapy and warm. She reaches for the washcloth, her fingers trailing over my chest as she gently scrubs me.

I close my eyes.

I'm lost in her touch.

She moves lower, and I feel myself growing harder with each passing second. Her fingers wrap around me, stroking me slowly and deliberately, and I gasp.

I lean into her, our bodies pressing together as the water continues to rain down on us.

Alina's lips find mine, *and we kiss deeply.*

I lose myself in the sensation of her body against mine, the warmth of her skin, the wetness of her hair as it brushes against my chest.

Alina breaks away from me suddenly, her eyes downcast. "I'm sorry," she whispers, "I don't want to touch you in any way that will hurt."

I reach out to her, my hand finding her cheek and gently lifting her face so our eyes meet. "You are not hurting me."

With a tender touch, I run my thumb over her bottom lip before closing the distance between us.

Our lips meet.

A soft sigh escapes her as our bodies press together.

I deepen the kiss, my tongue seeking out hers as I pull her closer.

The bruises on my body may ache...

But now, with her in my arms...

I feel alive and whole.

●

Alina turns off the shower and helps me step out, wrapping a towel around me. I wince as I try to move my fingers, my injuries making even the simplest tasks difficult. But she is patient as she helps dry me off.

Once I'm dry, she leads me to the bed, helping me ease onto the soft mattress. She sits beside me, taking my hand and placing it on her thigh.

"I want to make you feel good," she murmurs, leaning in to kiss my lips softly. "Just let me take care of you."

She takes my injured hand, pressing soft kisses to my fingertips. With her other hand, she trails her fingers down my chest as I watch her slide down my body, her lips pressing gentle kisses to my skin.

The pain fades away as I focus on the pleasure of her touch, the sensation of her lips on my skin.

"Alina," I gasp, my voice a hoarse whisper.

She looks up at me, her eyes shining. "Yes, Kane?"

"Please, don't stop."

A smile plays at the corner of her lips as she continues her ministrations, trailing her tongue along my skin.

My body responds eagerly to her touch, my desire for her growing with each passing second.

I reach up with my other hand, running my fingers through her hair and pulling her closer. Our lips meet again, hungry and passionate, as we explore each other's mouths.

As we break apart, I gaze into her eyes, "I want you, Alina," I whisper. "I need you."

With a soft touch, Alina runs her fingers through my hair and caresses my face before placing a gentle kiss on my lips. "I want you too," she whispers. She pulls back slightly, looking into my eyes, "I was so scared that I was going to lose you," her voice cracking, "I don't want to lose you."

I reach up to touch her face, my thumb brushing her lips. "You won't lose me," I assure her, pulling her in for another kiss.

She moves down my body, her lips trailing kisses over my chest and stomach until she reaches my length. I gasp as she takes me into her mouth, the warmth and wetness driving me wild.

Despite my injuries, I thrust into her mouth, seeking more of her touch. Alina moves her head up and down, taking me deeper with each stroke.

I moan her name.

My fingers tangle in her hair as my pleasure builds.

With one last flick of her tongue, I reach the edge, exploding into her mouth with a guttural groan that makes my body ache.

CHAPTER SEVENTEEN

I slowly slip out of bed, careful not to wake Alina.

My body aches as I make my way downstairs to find Stian cleaning his guns. He looks at me and asks, "How'd you sleep?"

I nod in response and approach him. Stian has always been loyal to Nikolai but risked everything to save me.

"Thank you for everything, Stian," I say, "I know what you did to save me wasn't easy, and it put you in danger."

Stian shrugs, setting aside his gun. "Nikolai's not the man he used to be," he says bitterly, "Putting his men and Alina in danger just to take you down was a low move."

"I owe you my life."

Stian looks at me, "You owe me nothing," he says firmly. "You are the closest I have to a family, Kane. And family looks out for each other."

"What happens now?" I ask.

Stian takes a deep breath, "We wait," he says. He then looks at me and gives me a side-eye, a sly smirk playing at the corner of his lips. "So, about the princess..." he teases.

I raise an eyebrow, knowing exactly where this is going. "What about her?"

Stian chuckles, "I remember when you said nothing was going on between you two because you knew how to do your job. Your job was to protect her, not fuck her."

I let out a deep sigh, "Yeah, I remember."

"But now," Stian continues, "you've fallen for her, haven't you?"

I don't respond.

I don't want to give him the satisfaction of an answer.

Stian shakes his head, "I don't blame you, Sullivan. She's a catch and has you wrapped around her finger."

I scowl, "She's not some object to be caught."

"All right, all right. I get it," Stian says, "It's not like it matters anymore. There's no way we are going back to the Moskal mansion. You are not her bodyguard anymore."

I hear Alina coming down the stairs, and I look to see her wearing one of my oversized shirts, which covers her torso but shows off the length of her legs.

"Good morning," she greets us with a smile before walking over to me and hugging me from behind, planting a soft kiss on my cheek.

She moves on to the kitchen, and Stian teases, "I think it's rude not to give me a kiss of good morning as Kane got."

I quickly interject, "Watch it, Evensen."

"Do you have coffee?" Alina asks, ignoring Stian's comment.

"I have coffee, but I doubt you know how to brew some."

"You would be surprised," she says, rummaging through the cabinets.

I watch her, admiring the way the shirt drapes over her curves.

My thoughts are interrupted when Alina faces us and asks, "What are we going to do about my father?"

Stian looks at her, then me, and back to her again. "I didn't exactly have a plan when I took off to go help Kane yesterday," he admits.

"We need to be careful," I say, "Nikolai won't let this go. He'll come after us with everything he's got."

"He will have no problem killing me if needed," Alina says.

Stian shakes his head, "Nikolai would never kill you, Alina. Make you watch Kane being tortured and killed? Sure, but he would never kill his princess."

Alina's face turns pale, "He killed my mother."

Stian looks at her, "That was different. Yes, Nikolai killed his wife, but he would never touch a hair on your head. He may be many things, but he loves you, Alina. Even if it doesn't look like it sometimes."

"Love?" she scoffs. "Is that what you call it? Making me shoot people, forcing me to be a part of something I don't want to, never letting me have a normal life?"

Stian stops for a second, taken aback by her outburst, and Alina continues, her arms crossed in front of her.

"Do you think it's easy being 'the princess'?" she asks, "Do you think my life is painted in gold?"

Stian shakes his head. "No, Alina. I know it's not like that, and that's not what I was trying to say."

Alina interrupts him again. "I've seen more people being killed and tortured than you could ever imagine. My father made me do things, things that still haunt me to this day. He wanted to protect my body but never tried to protect my soul.

He believed I needed to do those things to be strong and know how to live in this world."

I notice Alina is shaking.

I reach out and take her arm, pulling her towards me so she faces me. I take her hand in mine and pull her closer, trying to give her some comfort.

Stian continues, "I know all of that, Alina. I know it because I've seen it happen. I know Nikolai's orders to every man, and I was there with you most of the time. But I also know that Nikolai would never touch you. And if you were in real danger yesterday, he would give his body for yours."

"Were you there when my father killed my mother?" Alina asks.

Stian avoids her gaze and doesn't reply.

Alina chuckles bitterly. "You were, weren't you?"

Stian finally looks her in the eye and nods.

"Alina," I start to say, but she interrupts me by bursting into tears, covering her face with her hands.

Alina's body tenses up as she starts shaking her head. Without thinking, I pull her gently towards me so she sits on my leg, and I wrap my arm around her waist, wanting to comfort her.

"And you did nothing to stop it?" she asks Stian, her voice muffled by her sobs.

"What did you want me to do, Alina? I didn't agree with everything your father did, not even with half of it, okay? But your father's orders are rules... if he was doing that to your mother, what do you think he would do to me if I crossed him?"

Alina shouts, "She was my mother!"

"I know," Stian replies.

Alina asks him, tears streaming down her face, "Were you part of it? Did you touch her?"

Stian shakes his head. "I never touched her. I was just there... watching and guarding the door."

Alina loses it and gets up, pacing around the room. "Why couldn't you cross my father to save my mother, but you did it yesterday for me?"

"I didn't do it for you, Alina. I did it for Kane."

Alina keeps her eyes on Stian's, "What do you mean?"

Stian takes a deep breath before answering. "I mean that I was not your bodyguard, Alina. My duty was to protect your father, not you. And I told you before, Nikolai would never hurt you."

Alina looks at me, searching for answers in my eyes.

But I remain silent.

Stian takes a moment to continue, "I did what I did yesterday because I knew Kane didn't stand a chance if I didn't do anything. And I couldn't let that happen."

"What kind of relationship do you have that makes you betray my father?" she searches between Stian and me.

"I will tell you everything if you want. Can you please sit down a bit?" That's when I reach out and touch her hand gently.

Alina looks at me and nods, sitting next to me.

●

"I met Stian when I was on the streets," I say, looking into Alina's eyes while she holds my hand. "Years ago, before I

121

worked for your father, I used to do... a lot of stuff. Anything that would pay for food or make me survive out there in the middle of people worse than your father," I continue. "I used to street fight, people would come and pay for fights to happen, and I won all the time. That was my best source of income. Until one day, Stian came into the picture."

I pause for a moment, taking another deep breath.

"He gave me money for a fight, but not just any fight. He paid me to fight with him." I say, "We gave it all we had, but neither of us could take the other down. Stian talked to me after the fight and told me that I had some talent and that the things I could do could take me far in life. He said he knew some people that could help me go places." I pause before resuming, "Stian left and returned after a few days to take me to Nikolai, and that's how it all started."

Alina interrupts me, her voice trembling. "When did you start working for my father?"

"I started some years ago," I reply, "but I never went to the mansion much until now when I was hired to protect you. That's why you remember seeing me around, but not much."

"What kind of job were you doing for my father?" she asks.

"You know what kind of job I was doing, Alina," I tell her, "I was doing the dirty work, killing and torturing... that's all I knew before I was called to go to the mansion and was assigned to be your bodyguard."

"Okay, back to your relationship with Stian," Alina says, bringing me back to the present.

I take a deep breath before continuing. "When I started working for Nikolai, it was hard to gain his trust. So, for all the jobs I was assigned, Stian was also there, ordered to watch and never help. That's how we started spending a lot of time together. Eventually, I taught him some of the fighting techniques I learned on the streets, and he showed me how to handle guns perfectly. We got better and learned from each other."

I pause momentarily.

"Nikolai never knew anything was happening between us. He would never tolerate any bond between his men, so we made it look like we barely knew each other. But the truth is, we started working together on the jobs and getting closer. We no longer had any family, so it wasn't hard to start seeing each other as brothers."

I take a deep breath before continuing.

"So, one day, we promised each other that the only reason we would ever betray Nikolai was to save each other's lives. And that's what happened."

CHAPTER EIGHTEEN

Stian's phone rings, and he answers right away.

From where I stand, I can't hear what the person on the other end is saying. He listens carefully, nodding before finally saying, "Noted," and hanging up.

Alina and I exchange a look, both of us curious about what Stian has just heard. He doesn't keep us waiting long, "Nikolai is back at the mansion. The security has been amped up, and they're actively looking for us.".

"How do you know that?" Alina asks.

"Let's just say I have someone on the inside who's keeping tabs," Stian replies.

"Other men are betraying my father?"

"Not exactly a betrayal," Stian says, hesitating momentarily. "I met someone from the outside who could easily be on the inside without anyone noticing."

Alina looks at Stian, "Explain."

Stian leans forward, resting his arms on his knees. "Years ago, I met a woman who used to do small jobs for Nikolai. She isn't part of the staff or the 'clan' per se, but she has access to the inside. We got... close... and she still goes in and out without arousing suspicion. She has eyes inside, and Nikolai will never suspect a thing."

"So, what do we do now?" I ask.

"We need to be careful," Stian replies, looking at Alina and me. "He doesn't know we are informed, but if he has men looking for us, it won't take long until they find us here. We are too close."

•

I clench my teeth, feeling the sharp pang in my chest with each movement as I bend down to pack my clothes into the backpack Stian gave us.

Alina spots my discomfort and hurries to my side.

"Are you okay?" she asks.

"I'm fine," I try to keep my voice steady.

She gently places a hand on my shoulder and looks into my eyes. "You are not fine, Kane. Let me help you."

I won't argue with her.

I let her take over.

We finish packing our essentials and zip up the bags. Stian appears at the door, looking impatient.

"Are you two done yet? We need to leave."

"We are ready," Alina replies, grabbing her backpack.

Stian hands me mine, and we make our way out of the room and towards the exit.

"We're heading to my hometown," I tell Alina as we pile into the car. "It's far enough away from here to buy us some time."

"Got it," she nods, fastening her seatbelt.

Stian starts the engine, and we drive in silence.

I focus on my breathing, trying to ignore the pain, while Alina stares out the window, lost in her thoughts.

After what seems like hours, we finally arrive at my hometown. Stian parks the car a few feet from the house, wanting to avoid drawing any unwanted attention to our presence.

I wince as I stand up from the car seat, and Stian helps me out, with Alina following suit. We approach my childhood home, which looks smaller than I remember, and the front yard is overgrown with weeds.

The porch desperately needs repair, with the railing barely holding on.

I examine the front door carefully, looking for a way to get inside without breaking it down. After a few moments, I find the hidden latch and push it to release the lock.

"Is this your house?" Alina asks, peering around.

I nod, "Yeah, we used to live here." The door swings open silently, and I motion for Alina and Stian to follow me inside.

I take a deep breath as I step inside the house.

Dust covers every surface.

Untouched since the day my parents were killed.

Alina's voice breaks the silence, "You and your parents?"

I pause, looking around the space, and reply, "And Klara."

Alina touches my arm, and Stian closes the door behind us. "This place is surely enough to buy us some time."

I walk through the house, backpack on my back, with Alina silently following me.

I open the kitchen cabinets.

I move the chairs.

… I just look around.

Everything reminding me of my parents.

The memories flooding my mind.

The sound of my parent's laughter and the sight of their lifeless bodies on the living room floor all come rushing back, causing a lump in my throat.

My gaze shifts to the living room floor, and I notice the blood stain on the wood.

It's still here.

Alina follows my gaze and looks at the floor. "What happened here, Kane?"

I don't look at her and say, "That's my parents' blood."

"I'm so sorry, Kane," Alina whispers.

I look away from the dried blood on the floor and meet her eyes. I put my backpack on the couch and go to the stairs.

I start to climb, my heart beating faster with every step. The memories flood back to me as I reach the first floor. I pause outside my old room, taking a deep breath before opening the door.

The room is just as I left it.

My old desk is cluttered with notebooks and pens.

My bed is unmade, just as I left it on the day I left.

Posters of my favorite bands still adorn the walls.

I walk around the room, taking it all in. Every corner holds a memory.

I'm transported to a time when everything was different.

When my parents were still alive.

When everything was normal.

But now, everything has changed.

I turn to face Alina, who has followed me into the room. She looks around, taking in my old space. "This was your room?"

I nod, unable to find my voice.

Alina steps closer to me, her hand resting on my arm. "Do you want to talk about it?"

I shake my head, knowing that I can't.

Not yet.

Not now.

●

We sit around the old wooden dining table, a lantern as our only light source since the electricity is out. The silence is broken only by spoons scraping against the tin of our canned soup. Stian analyzes a map on his phone, *his informant's intel on Nikolai's next move.*

Just then, we hear a sound coming from the back of the house. Stian looks at me, and I turn off the lantern.

"The house has two entrances. The sound is coming from the back one." I whisper as I motion for Alina to be quiet and hide behind the staircase wall in case things go south.

Stian grabs his gun, and I take my knife.

We communicate through gestures, *years of working together*, making our movements almost effortless. Stian goes one way, and I go the other, approaching the back entrance where the sound came from.

As I near the entrance, I see a shadow standing in the dark. I move around to hold the person against my body, knife at the ready.

As my eyes adjust to the dark, I see it's a woman.

Stian stops in front of us, gun pointed at her. I feel the woman's body tense up against mine. Her breaths are short and shallow, her hands shaking in the air as if to signal her surrender, "Please don't."

I keep my knife at her neck, feeling her swallow hard against the blade of my knife, her skin cool and smooth beneath my grip.

"Who are you?" I ask.

The woman hesitates before answering.

I press the knife closer to her neck. "Who are you?" I ask again.

Stian chimes in, "Are you with Nikolai?" He points the gun closer to her.

She shakes her head, saying, "I swear I have no clue who that guy is!"

I'm losing my patience, and Stian can see that.

"If I were you, I would start talking," he tells her. "My friend here is not very patient."

The woman takes a deep breath and says, "I used to live here. This was my home."

My grip on the knife loosens, and I step back.

"Lower your weapon, Stian," I say, my voice firm but calm.

Stian hesitates for a moment but eventually lowers his gun.

The woman exhales a deep breath.

"What's your name?" I ask.

"Klara," she says, her voice still shaky. "Klara Sullivan."

CHAPTER NINETEEN

I brush my hand through my hair and walk over to Stian's side. I look at her for a second, taking in her features.

This can't be real.

This girl can't be Klara.

Why would she be here today?

Why now?

"What are you doing here?" I ask.

She stutters a bit before replying, "I come here every now and then."

I don't wait to hear more and ask, "Why?"

And she replies, "Because this was my house."

"Why isn't it your house anymore?" I ask, trying to piece everything together and see if she knows the details.

The girl looks at me, trying to adjust her eyes in the dark to see me, and replies, "You have nothing to do with that."

I point my knife at her and reply, "Oh, but I do. So, you better answer my question."

She swallows and finally answers, "Because my parents were killed."

I lower the knife.

This can't be true.

There are many ways she may know about the killing.

It *doesn't mean she's Klara*.

I hear Alina behind me, "What's happening?"

I don't look at her, focusing solely on the girl in front of me.

"Are you throwing a party here or something?" The girl asks nervously.

Stian replies, "Something..."

I take a deep breath and ask her, "How old were you when your parents were killed?"

I need to be sure this girl is not lying.

I need to make sure we are not being tricked.

"What the fuck?" she says.

Stian's gun clicks as he points the gun at her. "Answer the fucking question."

The girl finally says, "I was six, jeez."

I nod.

Can she be Klara?

I ask her one more question, "And how old are you now?"

She takes a second but finally replies, "I'm twenty-six."

Shit.

It could be her.

I was fourteen, and Klara was six the day those men came into this house and killed our parents for nothing.

It's been twenty years since that day.

Stian still has his gun pointed at her, and Alina stands behind me, looking at us. I rub my face in frustration and finally walk up to the girl and stop before her.

It's so dark that I can't even see her face clearly.

Without a word, I grab her arm and pull her along with me toward the living room.

She screams, "Let go of me!"

But I don't listen.

I need to know the truth.

Alina calls out to me, "Kane, stop! What are you doing?" but I don't pay attention.

Stian follows us, keeping his gun trained on the girl.

I stop in front of the chair where my backpack is and reach inside it. By now, the girl has stopped screaming, "Kane?" she repeats my name.

"Yeah, Kane..." I mutter.

I turn on the lamp on the table and take a picture of Klara from my backpack when she was six years old.

The girl looks at me, her big grey eyes filled with shock, as I throw the picture of Klara on the table and ask, "Who is that?"

She looks at the picture.

Then she looks back at me.

I see a tear streaming down her face before she replies, "That's me. That's me when I was six."

My heart races as I realize that she is telling the truth.

My sister is alive and standing right in front of me.

The world around me fades into the background as a whirlwind of emotions engulfs me.

Klara is alive...

After all these years, my sister... *my little sister is alive.*

Alina's voice calling me is distant, barely registering in my mind. I'm drawn to this girl, my sister, standing there with tear-filled eyes.

I close the distance between us and reach for her, my arms instinctively wrapping around her, pulling her into a tight embrace. It's a hug that carries twenty years' worth of longing, pain, and unanswered questions.

I hold her tightly, never wanting to let go.

The realization that my sister, whom I believed to be lost forever, is alive and standing in my arms is overwhelming. Tears well up in my own eyes.

Relief.

Joy.

The weight of all the time we've lost.

"It's really you," I whisper, "After all this time, you're here."

•

We've been sitting on the couch for an eternity. Alina stands near me while I sit in front of Klara, with Stian beside me. Klara looks at me like she's trying to take all the information in.

"You really are Kane…." Klara finally manages to say.

I nod slowly, not taking my eyes off her.

"I thought you were dead," she tells me, closing her eyes and letting a tear escape.

I don't know what to say or do.

That's when Alina comes in and says, "So, let me see if I get it. You are Kane's sister?"

Klara looks at her and nods before saying, "I am."

"You are indeed similar. Your hair is pretty much the same color, and your eyes are exactly the same," Alina adds.

I get up from the couch and put my hands on the back of it, trying to get some distance. "Where were you all this time?"

She stays seated and hesitates. "I… I was adopted not long after what happened."

I scoff and reply, "I looked everywhere for you! I looked everywhere, Klara... you were nowhere to be found."

She shuts her eyes momentarily and says, "I was adopted by a couple who couldn't have kids. They gave me everything I could ask for." I start pacing around, and she asks, "What about you?"

I stop, look at her, and say, "I lived on the streets," making her clearly uncomfortable. "No one adopts a fourteen-year-old kid. I stayed there until I was old enough to be on my own, and then I went to the fucking streets to make a life for myself. That's what's about me."

"I'm sorry," Klara says, her voice shaking. "I never knew what happened to you after that day."

"It's not your fault. I'm glad you got a family to love you."

She looks at me with tears in her eyes and says, "Kane, I never got to thank you for protecting me that day."

I'm taken aback by her words as she continues.

"I am alive thanks to you, and I don't remember seeing mom and dad dying because I only remember your shirt, from how you held me against you, not letting me see anything."

I look down, *remembering pieces of that moment.*

I remember holding my hands against Klara's ears as the men beat my parents' bodies with the baseball bat. I remember having Klara against my chest as my mom looked at me for the last time, ensuring we were hidden enough not to be seen and suffer the same fate they did.

"You were just a kid," I finally manage to say.

Alina moves to my side and holds my hand, trying to find my eyes. "Kane, I'm so sorry. I had no idea."

I look at her and then at Klara again. "It's in the past. I don't want to think of that anymore."

Klara wipes a tear from her eye before changing the topic, "But what are you doing here, then?"

Stian answers her, "We are hiding."

Klara looks at Stian and asks, "Hiding from who?"

Alina answers, "From my father."

"The guy you asked me for when you held weapons against me?" Klara asks, her eyes flickering between us.

Stian speaks up, "Yeah, sorry about that. We didn't know you were a Sullivan."

"Why are you hiding, though?"

"Because if he finds me, I'm a dead man," I tell her bluntly.

"Because you and his daughter are a thing?" she asks, directing her gaze towards Alina.

"Sort of," Alina says.

"It's a long story..." I add.

"I have time," Klara smiles at us.

•

I sit across from Alina and Klara, watching as the two of them chat away.

We've been here for hours.

We've been telling Klara everything that happened these last few days, from my assignment as Alina's bodyguard to Nikolai torturing me.

Klara looks visibly shocked, her eyes wide as she listens intently. "Shit, this is literally mafia business?"

Alina inhales deeply before replying, "Looks like it."

Klara's eyes widen even more. "You are, like, the mafia princess or something?"

Alina looks at Klara and says, "Please don't call me that."

"Sorry," Klara says sheepishly.

"We are hoping to stay here for some time. Nikolai is looking for us, and it's dangerous to get back right now," I explain.

Klara gets up suddenly, "Well, I can bring you some goods for the time you are here, I'll go home, and I will bring you some things to make you comfortable enough for the time you are here!"

"Thank you," I say.

"And if you need to shower, you can come to my house," Klara adds.

I immediately shake my head, "Being so close to us puts you at risk, and I don't want that. We'll manage. Thank you."

Klara approaches me, her gaze unwavering, "Kane, we've been through so much. We're family, and I don't want to be separated from you now that I've finally found you again. I understand the risks, but I want to help."

"Klara, you have no idea how much it means to me that you want to be there for us. But the truth is, it's too dangerous for you to be so close. The people after us won't hesitate to use anyone I care about as leverage. I can't bear the thought of something happening to you."

Klara's voice softens, "I appreciate your concern, Kane, but...."

Stubborn girl...

I interrupt her, "I won't argue with you about this. It's not like we'll ever see each other again. We'll keep in touch, I promise. We'll find safe ways to communicate and stay connected. We will be together soon, just not in your house. Not that close to your personal space."

Klara pulls me into a tight hug.

I hold her close, "We'll figure it out, Klara," I whisper, "I swear."

Klara pulls back and nods, looking down at her feet before glancing back at Alina. "I'll be back with the goods," she says before leaving.

Once Klara is out of earshot, Alina turns to me. "She's sweet."

I nod and lean back in my chair.

CHAPTER TWENTY

Klara brought us some clean blankets and food, making our hideout more comfortable for the time being. My childhood bed is too small for Alina and me, and I refuse to sleep in my parents' bed. *In fact,* I hadn't even stepped inside their room since we arrived.

We put some blankets on the floor of my old room and pillows, and that's where Alina and I will sleep tonight. Stian insisted on sleeping on the couch to keep watch over the house in case it's necessary.

I lie on the floor, one arm up with my hand under my pillow, when Alina puts her hand on my chest and says, "I had no idea you went through all that, Kane. It's not fair for you."

I turn my head to face her, my eyes locking onto her beautiful eyes and long lashes, and pull her face to mine with the other hand, kissing her lips.

She then continues, "I'm sorry I made it look like my life was difficult, like I wasn't privileged. I spoke to you as if my life was chaos, but I was protected all my life while you fought for yours, God knows how."

I stop her, "Your life wasn't easy either, Alina. We had different paths, none of them easy. Both different, both broken."

"I'm sorry, Kane," she whispers, kissing my lips gently. "Do you know why it happened?"

I shake my head, "It was supposed to be a simple home invasion. Two men entered our house at night while we were asleep. My dad went downstairs when he heard the noise. My mom came to our rooms and told us to hide. Dad tried to fight the guys, and one of them hit his head and made him collapse. My mom tried to help him, and they started to get nervous. Klara heard my mom screaming and went downstairs, but I was able to hide her in time. We hid under the table and watched as everything happened."

Alina looks deep into my eyes, and then she closes them briefly. She holds my face and touches her nose to mine. "I really am sorry."

I push myself forward, placing my hands on her waist and pulling her towards me. She straddles my lap, her legs around my waist, and I run my hands over her back and down to her curves, making her lean in closer, grab my face, and kiss me deeply.

"Can you please help me not think about that anymore?" I ask her.

Alina nods and gives me a soft smile, "Of course," she says before leaning in for another kiss. She then breaks the kiss, "I don't want to move too much and hurt you," she says, making me smile.

I put a strand of her hair behind her ear and say, "I'm okay, princess."

She smiles and leans in for another kiss.

I deepen the kiss, and my hands roam over her body, tracing her curves and contours.

I break the kiss and move my lips down her neck.

Alina moans softly while my tongue laves over her skin. Her hands tangle in my hair, pulling me closer to her, urging me on. I oblige, letting my hands wander over her body.

I kiss down to her collarbone, tracing circles over her sensitive skin. Alina's hands grip my shoulders tightly as I explore her body, my lips moving lower and lower.

I reach the top of her top and slide my hands underneath, feeling the soft skin of her stomach. Alina arches her back, pushing her chest forward, giving me better access. I take the hint, kissing my way down to her breasts, tracing the outline with my tongue, feeling her nipples harden under my touch.

"Kane," Alina moans, her hands roaming over my back, pulling me closer to her.

I tease her with my mouth, taking one nipple and sucking gently before switching to the other.

The taste of her skin and the sounds she makes are driving me crazy.

I move my hands down to the hem of her skirt, my fingers sliding underneath and tracing the outline of her thighs. Alina's breath hitches as my fingers brush against the lace of her panties, and I can feel the heat radiating off her body.

I'm lost in the moment.

Consumed by my desire for her.

I break the kiss and look down at her. Without a word, I pull her up, switching places so she's lying on the ground and I'm on top of her.

I ease her skirt down her hips, and she tosses her top aside, revealing her perfect body.

My mouth waters at the sight of her.

I move lower, planting kisses along her stomach and down to her hips. I tease the lace of her panties with my teeth, pulling them down slowly, savoring the anticipation. When they're finally off, I inhale the scent of her arousal.

I won't be able to hold back for long.

I run my tongue along the inside of her thigh, savoring the taste of her skin. Alina moans softly and arches her back, her hands gripping my shoulders as I move back up her body, and our lips meet again in a fiery kiss.

I want her more than anything.

I know she wants me just as badly.

I pull back slightly, gazing at her with dark, intense eyes. "I want you."

She nods, and I position myself between her thighs, my hands gripping her hips tightly as I enter her slowly. Alina gasps, her nails digging into my back as I move, the heat between us growing more and more intense with each passing second.

I feel Alina's muscles clench around me as I thrust deeper into her.

Her eyes flutter shut as I set a fast pace.

M hips slam into hers over and over again.

I take her breasts in my hands, kneading them and teasing her nipples with my fingers. Alina arches her back, her body writhing underneath me as she becomes lost in the pleasure.

My fingers trail down her body, finding their way between her legs as I thrust into her.

She's wet and ready for me.

I can feel her getting close.

Her breaths become more labored, and her moans louder.

I can't hold back any longer.

I feel the tension building within me, the need to release overwhelming. With one final thrust, I come as she arches her back and lets out a cry.

I continue to move within her, prolonging her pleasure until she's completely spent.

I collapse on her side, catching my breath.

Alina looks up at me with a soft expression. "Kane..."

I turn to face her, "Yes, princess?"

"I love you," she says softly.

My heart skips a beat at her words, "Alina..."

"I understand," she interrupts me, her expression falling slightly.

"Alina," I repeat, taking her face in my hands, "I love you too."

CHAPTER TWENTY-ONE

I walk into the kitchen, and Stian is sitting at the table, cutting and eating an apple.

"Had fun last night, uh?" Stian asks, a smirk planted on his lips as he looks at the apple.

I don't reply, and he continues.

"Thin walls."

I roll my eyes and grab an apple, cleaning it with my hand and biting into it, sitting in front of him. "Any news?"

"Waiting for Ari to call," Stian says.

"Who?" I ask.

Stian looks at me and realizes what he just said, looking down again.

"Oh, she has a name, I see."

Stian clears his throat and replies, "She was supposed to give me news by now..."

"Are you worried?"

"About what?"

"Your friend, Evensen."

"Not about her exactly, more about her being essential right now to not be caught by Nikolai's men... without her information, we are in the dark," he says.

"We can't run forever, Stian."

"If they caught her, by any chance, we are screwed, Sullivan. She is helping us. They won't take long to find us after that."

"How much does she know about us right now?"

"A lot."

"A lot, as in, where we are?" I ask him.

"Not the exact location, but she knows we are out of town."

I nod and look around before saying, "If she doesn't call you by noon, we worry, all right?"

"Morning," Alina says, coming downstairs and kissing me.

"Morning," Stian replies. "I will never get used to the fact that I don't get a morning kiss as well."

Alina walks over to him and kisses him on the forehead. "Happy now?" she smiles and goes for an apple.

That's all we have right now besides some canned soup, canned tuna, water, and bread, which is a lot, *thanks to Klara.*

Stian chuckles and says, "Could have been better."

"Again, Evensen, watch it." I point at Stian, who laughs in response.

Alina turns to Stian and asks, "What's the plan for today?"

Stian shrugs, "No plan. We are waiting for news from your home sweet home."

She glances at him and adds, "Your informant?" Alina leans against the counter and bites into her apple, asking, "Have you tried to call her?"

Stian shakes his head and says, "You don't know much about not leaving tracks, do you?"

"She's got a point, Stian," I tell him, "After all, Ari is using that phone to call you, right? So, there goes your plan of not leaving tracks."

Stian takes a deep breath and takes his phone, dialing a number and waiting for the call to be picked up.

Nothing.

No one picks up the call.

"Nothing," Stian says, looking at the phone before trying again.

We wait a bit.

Still nothing.

Stian starts looking worried.

He swallows and looks at me.

"She's not picking up."

"Maybe she's busy?" Alina suggests.

Stian looks at her and gets up. "If she doesn't return the call in an hour, I'm going to the mansion."

"Hey, easy... You are going nowhere alone," I say.

Stian looks at me and says, "Watch me."

As I am about to reply, his phone rings.

He looks at the screen and automatically answers. "Ari,"

His expression changes as he puts his phone on speaker. "Mr. Evensen, long time no see," Nikolai says, making Stian bite his lip and clench his jaw. "Are you done playing hide and seek? The three of you?"

Stian doesn't reply.

Nikolai chuckles and says, "I will assume my daughter is there listening to this, so I will speak to her."

I look at Alina, who is dead staring at the phone in Stian's hand.

None of us say anything, and Nikolai continues talking. "Alina, darling. Come home... there's still time, there's still a place for you, and this time, because it's the first time, there will be no consequences for you."

He finishes talking, and Alina says, "Screw you."

Nikolai takes a deep breath on the other side of the phone. "There, there... that's no way of speaking to your father, is it now?"

"After what you did?" she asks.

"I did nothing to you, Alina. Don't be such a drama queen..." Alina shakes her head and doesn't reply.

"Where's Ari?" Stian asks.

"Ah, Mr. Evensen, right," Nikolai says. "Ari... we are talking about your little elf, right? Santa's little helper?"

Stian closes his fist, trying to control his anger.

"Well... she's... alive."

"What did you do to her?" Stian asks him.

"Me? Nothing... but my men are less patient than I am. So, when they found out that she was snitching... let's say they are not the sweetest people in this world."

Stian's eyes turn red, and I finally speak. "What do you want, Nikolai?"

Nikolai laughs, "Mr. Sullivan, finally the man I wanted to hear."

"What do you want?" I repeat.

"Two things only, Mr. Sullivan. I want my daughter back under my roof, and I want you dead."

"No deal," Alina says.

"This is not a democracy, Alina," Nikolai says.

"What about Ari?" I ask.

"What about her?" Nikolai says.

"Are you letting her go?"

Nikolai laughs, "Of course not, Kane. Come on... you are smarter than that. She will die, just as you will, as soon as I land my hands on you."

"You are not a very good negotiator, are you, Mr. Moskal?" Stian asks.

"I never said I was up for negotiation," Nikolai spits. "And Alina, you are coming home. It was never a choice. The choice is between coming home without any consequences or my men bringing you home... and you know they are not so kind." Nikolai says before hanging up.

I clench my fists as the call ends, and Alina asks quietly, "What are we going to do?"

"We are not going to let him take you," I say firmly, my eyes locked onto hers. "We'll figure something out."

Stian stands a few feet away, looking lost in thought, "He has Ari."

•

I sit at the table with Stian and Alina, my eyes scanning the maps and notes in front of us.

We've been planning for hours, trying to find a way to rescue Ari from the clutches of Nikolai and his men.

"We need to move quickly," Stian says. "Nikolai knows we are coming."

"We know where she is," I state matter-of-factly. "That place, we've seen it countless times."

I shift my gaze to Alina.

"Whenever Nikolai wants to make someone pay for their deeds, he takes them there. Stian and I can vouch for that. And he wants us to come and rescue her, so he is obviously holding her somewhere he knows we are going to look." I look back at the map and add, "We just have to find a way to get in and out without being noticed immediately."

Stian looks up, "I might have an idea," he says. "We could use the old tunnels," he adds, pointing to a series of lines on the map. "They're abandoned now, but they used to connect the building where Ari is being held. If we can find a way in through the tunnels, we might be able to avoid detection."

"It's risky," I say, "but it might be our best chance."

"Okay, when are we leaving?" Alina asks.

"You are staying, Alina," I tell her.

Alina's eyes narrow as she steps forward. "I'm coming with you."

I shake my head. "No, you're not."

"Why not?" she demands, crossing her arms over her chest.

Stian chimes in, "It's too dangerous, Alina. You need to stay here."

"I'm not a child, Stian," she retorts, glaring at him before returning her attention to me. "I can help. I can be useful."

"It's not a good idea," I tell her firmly.

"Why not?" she persists.

I hesitate for a moment, searching for the right words. "You'll do more bad than good if you come with us."

Alina swallows and looks down for a moment before nodding. "Sure."

I run my hand through my hair. "Alina, that's not what I meant," I say, moving towards her and reaching out to touch her hand.

But she shoves it off, "Forget it, do whatever you please."

I look to Stian for help, but he nods and says, "We need to move."

I nod, "Stay safe," I say, looking at Alina.

She doesn't look at me and doesn't say anything back.

I look at Alina before turning and following Stian out of the room.

I know I made the right call...

But that doesn't make it any easier to leave her behind.

•

I check the guns, ensuring they are loaded and ready for action.

Stian is already in the driver's seat, waiting for me to hop in. But before I can even get in the car, Alina runs towards us.

"Wait!"

I turn around.

She reaches me and throws her arms around me, "I don't want you to go, Kane."

Holding her tightly, I kiss her head, "I have to help Stian, princess."

"If my father finds you, he will finish what he started," she says, tears forming in her eyes.

"He won't. I'll be careful."

"Kane, please don't die. I can't lose anyone else I love through my father's hands."

Someone she loves.

These words, I won't ever get used to them.

"I am not dying," I take a deep breath and cup her face in my hands, lightly kissing her lips.

Alina tears and says, "Please, let me go with you. I don't want to be here by myself either."

I nod, understanding her fear but knowing it's unsafe for her to come with us.

"I know, Alina, but it's too risky. Your father knows we are coming and expects you to come as well. We can't give him that."

Alina shakes her head, "But there must be a way."

"Alina, if you come, your father will do whatever it takes to get you back and probably won't even blink at killing Ari, Stian, and me. I hate to say this, but we can use you as leverage in this situation."

Alina tightens her grip around me and nods resolutely.

"You're right."

I look around, thinking for a moment.

"What if you call Klara? She can stay with you while we are gone. You will be safe with her."

Alina sniffles and nods, her tears streaming down her face.

"Okay."

"I'll be back soon," I tell her.

"You promise?"

"I promise," I say firmly, trying to reassure her and myself that everything will be alright.

CHAPTER TWENTY-TWO

I leave the car and look around, scanning the area for any signs of Nikolai or his men.

My phone rings, and I answer it without hesitation.

It's Nikolai.

"It took you long enough," he sneers, "But I see you finally made it."

Obviously, he was expecting us to come for Ari.

And he's enjoying every minute of it.

This man loves to play games.

He loves to make us dance to his tune.

I grit my teeth, not wanting to give him the satisfaction of knowing he got under my skin.

"Where's Ari?" Stian demands.

"She's not dead... for now," Nikolai says. "But I don't see Alina with you. Where is she?"

I let out a humorless laugh. "You think I'm that stupid? I'd never bring Alina to you again."

Nikolai's voice turns deadly serious. "You're playing with fire, Mr. Sullivan."

I scoff. "I'll die before letting you touch Alina again."

"You underestimate me, Kane. I will do whatever it takes to get what I want."

Stian steps forward, his face set in a cold, hard mask, "If you kill us, you'll never get to her. So, I guess that's not an option."

Nikolai laughs. "I never said I wanted to kill you, Stian. But I have no problem torturing you until I get the necessary information."

Stian bristles beside me, his grip tightening on his gun.

I warn Stian, silently telling him to keep his cool.

We need to play this smart if we want to get Ari back.

Nikolai speaks up again, addressing Stian. "Mr. Evensen, I think I can convince you to talk without torturing you, though." He then continues, "If you turn slightly, you'll be able to see an open door in the building. It's not guarded or anything. You can just come in and find your friend."

Stian replies, "Do you think I'm stupid, Nikolai?"

Nikolai's voice takes on a mocking tone. "Your friend is waiting for you, Mr. Evensen. I just don't know for how long."

And with that, he hangs up.

"That bastard," Stian seethes as I put my phone away. "He's playing games with us."

"He wants us to split up," I say.

Stian takes a deep breath, "He said there's an open door in the building."

I shake my head. "I don't know. I'm sure it's a trap. But we can't just leave Ari there."

He nods, "Let's move."

We start towards the building, guns ready, scanning the area.

"Wait, we need a plan. We can't just go for it." I tell Stian.

"What should we do then?"

"We can't simply go through that door without a plan. Nikolai is probably with his men in there. We know better than that, Stian. We need a distraction." I tell him.

"Okay." Stian says, "So, we need to make him think we are falling under his trap?"

I nod and tell him, "I'm sure he wants me. This will be risky because I can be wrong, but right now, he wants me, not you... and Ari is just a way to get to us. He doesn't want to catch you because he doesn't want to kill you. You didn't touch his daughter. So, we are both going in and pray that I'm right. When we get there, if he's there with his men, you leave, and if I'm right, he won't try to get you... he'll want me, and only me."

"You are crazy, Sullivan. If you are right, Nikolai will catch you and kill you."

"No, he won't. He needs to get to Alina... if he kills me, the chances of him getting Alina back are reduced to ashes."

"What if it doesn't work? What if you are wrong?"

I nod and reply, "If I'm wrong, I'll be a dead man soon enough."

"Kane, if this goes south..."

"It won't, okay?" I look at him and continue, "Trusting that I'm right, Nikolai will let you go. You run for your life and go look for Ari."

"Right, and you think Nikolai doesn't have men all over the place, including with Ari right now?"

I tilt my head and reply, "Of course he does. But I'm going to distract him, my friend. I will make sure I'll make a fuss. And I know you can deal with a few of Nikolai's men by yourself."

"Kane, you'll get yourself killed too fast that way," Stian starts pacing around.

I touch his shoulder and ask, "Stian, do you trust me?"

He stops and nods.

"Trust me here. Nikolai needs to know where Alina is. He won't kill me."

"But he can break you," Stian says.

"If he tries, that's when you come in." I tell him, "If you get to the car with Ari and I'm not there or don't show up in, let's say, thirty minutes, you come for me."

"Fucking hell, Sullivan... This is too risky. What if I get caught? I won't be able to go for you."

"Evensen, come on." I smile at him and start walking. "You are a tough man. Let's work this out together, like old times."

We approach the door.

Stian pushes the door open cautiously.

We step inside.

The room is dimly lit, with a faint smell of must and decay.

We move quickly, our footsteps echoing in the silence.

This noise.

A faint clicking sound.

Stian grabs my arm, and we freeze, listening intently.

The sound grows louder, and I realize the sound of guns being cocked.

"Go back, Stian," I say, "Get out of here. Find Ari. I'll hold them off."

Stian hesitates, "Kane, come on, man. I can't leave you here alone."

"You have to," I say firmly. "I'll be fine. Just go."

With a nod, Stian turns and sprints back towards the door.

I turn around slowly, my gun pointed forward, and come face to face with Nikolai and his men.

Nikolai is smirking, his gun aimed directly at me.

"I told you, Mr. Sullivan," he says. "You can't escape me."

Nikolai didn't make a move to stop Stian from leaving.

I was right.

•

Like a déjà vu, I once again sit in a chair with Nikolai standing before me, holding a gun.

But this time, he's not pointing it at me.

He is not beating me.

He is not doing anything.

He is simply looking at me.

"So, you're not killing me today?" I ask him, trying to get under his skin.

"Mr. Sullivan, don't rush this moment for me. It will happen in due time. Nothing to worry about."

"You realize that if you kill me, you'll never find Alina, and she'll never forgive you, right?"

Nikolai laughs bitterly, "Mr. Sullivan, I don't need my daughter's forgiveness." I can see the anger simmering under the surface of his calm exterior.

"She wanted to kill you." I provoke him further, "The day you decided to beat the hell out of me, Alina wanted to kill you. You should be thanking me you are alive, really."

Nikolai swallows, "No one ever told you to be more careful about what you say when you're tied up to a chair with an armed man in front of you?"

157

I scoff and reply, "Nikolai, you gain nothing if you kill me, and you know it. You want to make me pay for touching your daughter, but you have no idea where she is. You want to make me pay for taking her away from you, and that's the catch. I took her away from you, and you want her back, but there's no way she's coming back. I'm your only chance of finding her."

"You talk a big game, Mr. Sullivan. But you forget who's in charge here. You may have taken Alina away, but I'll get her back, with or without you."

"You're willing to risk your daughter's life for revenge, Nikolai?" I tease him. "That's a dangerous line to cross."

Nikolai leans in closer, his eyes darkening, "Don't you dare talk to me about lines to cross, Kane. You took my daughter and turned her against me. You think you are so high and mighty, but you're just a thug with a badge."

"You know what, Nikolai? You are right. I'm not a saint, but at least I'm not a monster like you. You're willing to hurt the people you love for your own selfish desires."

I keep trying to distract Nikolai as I work on releasing myself from the rope binding my hands.

I feel the fibers digging into my skin.

I can't let it show on my face.

I have to stay calm and focused.

"You can keep playing your games, Nikolai, but it won't change the fact that you are a monster. Alina knows the truth now and will never forgive you for what you've done. You lost her the day you decided to control her life."

I manage to wiggle my hand free from the rope, but I still have one hand bound.

I have to keep talking and buy myself more time.

Nikolai's eyes flicker, "You know nothing about me, Kane. You think you have the moral high ground..."

I interrupt him again.

"You turned your daughter against you with your twisted lies and control, and now you stand here, blaming me for your mistakes?"

"I did what I had to do to protect my family."

I smirk, "You keep telling yourself that, Nikolai. But deep down, you know that you made this mess yourself. And you're going to have to live with the consequences."

Nikolai steps closer to me.

His gun is still pointed at my head.

"I'll live with the consequences just fine, Kane. But you won't be around to see it."

CHAPTER TWENTY-THREE

I finally get free and wait for Nikolai to be distracted enough for me to act.

We hear gunshots, and Nikolai turns his head slightly, giving me the perfect opportunity to go for it. I lunge forward and grab Nikolai's gun, twisting it out of his grip.

"On your knees, Nikolai."

He's laughing, "Kane, I will never bend before you."

I scoff and press the gun harder against his forehead. "I think you should, Mr. Moskal."

Nikolai still doesn't move, so I grab his shoulder and force him to kneel before me.

He grunts in pain as his knee hits the ground. I keep the gun trained on him, not daring to let my guard down.

"You are a dead man, Kane."

I narrow my eyes, my finger tightening on the trigger. "No, Nikolai. You're the dead man."

"You don't understand the power I have, Kane. My associates won't let you get away with this."

I look at Nikolai and laugh, "I am not afraid of you, and I'm surely not afraid of your associates, Nikolai."

"What do you think will happen if you kill me, Kane?"

"The world will be a better place. I know that much."

"Mr. Sullivan, if you kill me, Alina is next in line. She'll be the new target, the main target. If she wasn't safe before, can you imagine how it will be from now on?" Nikolai says.

I unlock the gun's safety and press it closer to his skull.

"I was hired to protect her until now, and I will keep doing it. Your men will also be loyal to her. She doesn't need you."

Nikolai laughs and shakes his head, "Kane, don't be stupid. Alina doesn't have what it takes to lead."

That's your mistake, Nikolai.

You can't just talk about Alina like that.

I crouch before him and keep the gun trained on his head. "Shut your mouth, Nikolai. You need to take Alina's name out of your fucking mouth."

"If you kill me, Kane, you will also be a dead man. My men are loyal to me, even over my dead body. You kill me, and you will be nothing more than a corpse in a couple of minutes." Nikolai threatens.

I smile at him and reply, "Mr. Moskal, look around you."

He keeps his gaze on me.

I shout, "LOOK AROUND YOU!"

He looks around and licks his lip.

"Do you see your men here, Nikolai?"

His gaze returns to mine as he answers, "You are bluffing, Kane. You are in the same position I am right now. You have no clue if those gunshots mean Stian is alive or dead."

I shake my head. "You are wrong, Nikolai. I know exactly what's happening. Contrary to you, I believe in Stian's capacities."

"I wouldn't if I were you, Kane. You are dead if you do this."

He finally realizes I'm not playing games here.

"Didn't you say I would die either way, Nikolai? Come on. You are giving me mixed signals here."

"Kane, I know you. You are not that type of killer. You wouldn't kill me in cold blood." He says with a laugh.

I stare into his eyes and pull the trigger, watching Nikolai's lifeless body fall to the ground, "Oh, but I am."

I take a deep breath and stand up, wiping my hands clean.

It's done.

Nikolai Moskal is no more.

•

I walk through the corridor, my senses heightened and my heart racing with adrenaline.

It's eerily quiet now.

Except for my footsteps echoing against the walls.

Suddenly, a man comes running towards me and raises his gun, ready to shoot. I react quickly and raise my gun, prepared to fire.

"Nikolai is dead. Are you sure you want to die for a dead man?" I ask him firmly.

He hesitates momentarily, looking at me and then at the open door behind me.

"You want to go check for yourself?" I offer.

He glances back and forth between me and the door.

He is clearly unsure of what to do.

"I don't want to kill you. I don't want to kill anyone else over this shit. Don't make me."

He puts his finger on the trigger.

I shoot his arm, making him drop the weapon.

"Are you really willing to die?" I ask him, my eyes fixed on his.

"How did you do it?" The guy asks.

"Shot him in the head."

"How did you break free?" he asks.

"He was careless," I tell him, keeping my gun trained on him, "Your leader wasn't that good, see?"

I approach him, take his gun from the floor, and stare at him.

"Don't do anything stupid. I'm letting you go. Think about where your loyalty lies from now on," I warn him before turning around and walking away.

I can hear the man groaning in pain behind me.

I don't turn back.

I turn the corner with my gun drawn and ready for whatever may come my way.

I find myself staring down the barrel of another gun, but my lips turn up into a smile.

"Shit, Kane. I was about to go get you," he says, lowering his weapon.

"I knew you could do it, Stian," I pat him on the shoulder.

Behind Stian, there's a girl with long dark brown hair and brown eyes. She looks bruised but alive, and she's holding a gun.

Well, apparently, all women can use a gun nowadays.

Stian motions for her to put her weapon down and introduces me, "Ari, this is Kane, and we are leaving now before Nikolai finds a way of killing us."

"He won't," I say.

"What do you mean?" Stian asks.

"He's dead. I killed him," I tell him, walking past him.

Stian runs after me and asks, "Kane, you killed Nikolai?"

I stop and turn to him, "I shot him."

Stian blinks in disbelief.

"He was annoying me."

Stian shakes his head and says, "Kane, how do you plan on telling Alina that you killed her father?"

I take a deep breath and realize I don't know how to handle that situation.

"I don't know, Stian."

"Kane, I don't give a fuck that Nikolai is dead, okay? But he had people on his side..."

I interrupt him, "His place is Alina's now, Stian."

He shakes his head again, and I know he's about to protest. So, I quickly add, "Can we discuss this in the car? I don't want to shoot anyone else's arms today, and some of Nikolai's men still don't know he is dead. That makes us targets. And if someone else points their gun at me again today... I swear to God."

●

We enter the car, and Stian asks, "What's the plan?"

I look at him and reply, "What do you mean?"

"You killed Nikolai. What now?"

I take a deep breath and reply, "Alina takes over."

Stian chuckles and says, "Kane, Alina was never involved in her father's business, ever! She has no clue how to run the business. She can't protect herself against these people."

"That's why we are going to be there with her."

"Have you asked her if that's what she wants?"

I look away from him and reply, "Look, I didn't plan to kill him, okay? But he talked too much, and if he walked out alive... we would never stand a chance, Stian. It was something that needed to be done!"

"I couldn't care less that that bastard is dead, but I don't think you thought this through."

And he is right.

I didn't.

Alina wanted to kill her father the other day, but she was hot-blooded... it was something of the moment. *She didn't really want him dead.*

I stare out the window.

I've taken away Alina's father.

The only family she had left.

I have put her into a position she may not be ready for.

But I had to do it.

Nikolai was a liability. He would have destroyed us if he lived.

So, I destroyed him first.

CHAPTER TWENTY-FOUR

Alina rushes over to me and hugs me,

She holds me tight *and I return the hug, inhaling her scent.*

"I missed you," she says. "I was so scared you wouldn't come back."

Alina stands on her toes and presses her lips against mine. Her hands cup my face as she deepens the kiss.

I wrap my arms around her waist, pulling her closer.

While I can.

Eventually, we break apart, "Alina, we need to talk."

She looks up at me with wide eyes.

Stian closes the door after Ari enters, and Alina's gaze shifts to her before turning back to me.

Ari raises her hand slightly, and Alina smiles before walking over and saying, "You must be Ari. I'm glad you are okay! Thank you so much for all your help."

Stian takes Ari's arm and says, "We'll be upstairs. I need to check on Ari's wounds, and you two need to talk."

Then they disappear upstairs, leaving me and Alina in the living room.

I notice Klara sitting on the couch.

"I'm on my way out," she says.

"I didn't see you there before. I'm sorry."

"It's okay. I was keeping Alina some company." Klara smiles, touches Alina's arm, and walks to the door.

"Thank you, Klara," I say.

She nods and leaves.

As soon as the door closes and we are left alone in the living room, Alina hugs herself and asks, "What happened?"

I take a deep breath and sit on the couch before opening my mouth. "Alina... I did something."

She freezes in place, her eyes fixed on me. "What did you do, Kane?"

"I need to know something before I tell you."

"Kane..."

"How do you think all of this will end?" I ask her.

"What do you mean?"

"Your father is looking for us all over the place, and his men are also looking for us. What would you do if you had to find a way to stop it all?"

Alina stops for a moment before walking closer and sitting in front of me. "I don't know. Why, Kane?"

I look at her and say, "Alina, I need your honest answer here. What would you be willing to do to stop your father?"

My heart is pounding.

I know this will be hard for her to hear.

"Kane, what happened?" she asks, obviously worried.

I close my eyes briefly before finally saying, "Your father is dead."

Alina's mouth drops open, and her eyes turn red. "How?"

I don't reply, and she just knows.

"You killed him?"

I nod, not saying anything.

"You killed my father, Kane?" Her face changes to anger, and she walks up to me, slapping me. "You wouldn't let me do it, but you did it?"

I understand her anger.

"I wouldn't let you do it because you would have to live with that, with killing your father..."

"Who do you think you are, Kane?" she interrupts me.

"Alina, it was the only way, and you know it."

"Who decides that, Kane? You?"

I get up and stand before her, saying, "He killed your mother, Alina! He killed a lot of good people."

She interrupts me again, "So did you! Don't act like you're my knight in shining armor, Kane."

I exhale before replying, "I am not, and yes, I did. You are right. **But** he would kill me, Stian, and Ari one way or another..."

I watch as she paces in the living room.

"How did you do it?"

I shake my head, not wanting to reply.

"How did you do it, Kane?" she repeats.

"I shot him."

Alina closes her eyes, and a tear streams down her face. "I... I don't know what to tell you, Kane..."

She sits, and I crouch in front of her.

"No... don't even think about it." She leans back, getting away from me.

"I am not going to touch you, Alina."

She sniffles, "Why? Why did you kill him?"

"I am sorry..."

She looks at me, laughs bitterly, and says, "No, you are not."

And she's both right and wrong.

I'm not sorry I killed her father.

But I am sorry I made her feel this way.

•

We sit in silence for what feels like an eternity. Alina doesn't look at me, her eyes fixed on the view outside the window, tears streaming down her face.

Stian and Ari exchange occasional glances, but they remain quiet as well.

Finally, I break the silence, unable to bear it any longer. "What do you want to do now, Alina?"

Alina's head snaps towards me, "What? You don't have a plan for after killing my father, is that it?"

I know she's hurting.

I inhale deeply before speaking. "Do you want to go back?"

"To the mansion?"

"Yes, to the mansion."

"I'll get killed, Kane. Me, you, and everyone who comes close! Thanks to your actions, we are fucked," she spits out.

"No, we are not," I reply firmly. "You are your father's legacy, which means you are in charge now. These people are many things, but they are mostly loyal and respect hierarchy. So, if you are your father's successor, you are the one who gives orders now. I will only get killed if you order it."

Alina scoffs at my words, "Maybe I will."

Her words sting.

But I know she's lashing out because of her pain.

"You can do whatever you want, Alina."

"Okay, let's do it. We'll go back home." She says without thinking much.

"I know I haven't been in this game as long as you guys, but I can help too. I have training and experience in protecting things... and people." Ari says.

I glance at Stian, who nods before turning back to Ari. "Are you sure you want to do this?"

"Yeah, why not. I don't have anything else to do anyways," she smirks.

Alina takes over.

"Kane will always be with me as my bodyguard. Stian and Ari, I need you to help us with security while I talk to the rest of the men. I don't want anyone else to get hurt again." Her voice is firm, and I can see the determination in her eyes.

I nod.

Alina is getting the hang of it already.

"I need you to make sure no one attacks me as I speak to the men in the house. I must ensure they are all by my side and no one tries to kill me after my father's death."

"We will be there," I assure her.

"No one else dies today, Kane." She locks her eyes on mine.

I nod again, making her know that I understand.

Alina takes a deep breath, "Let the show begin."

CHAPTER TWENTY-FIVE

I keep my hand on my gun as we approach the mansion where Nikolai's men are stationed. Stian drives us through the gates, and immediately the men raise their guns.

I'm starting to think that this might be a suicide mission.

Stian parks the car, and the men yell at us to get out. I watch as Stian checks for his gun.

I can see uncertainty in Alina's eyes.

Alina gets out of the car and walks up to one of the men, Fabian, one of the leaders among Nikolai's men.

Without fear, I hear her saying, "How much do you know about the current situation, Fabian?"

Fabian keeps his gun trained on us but doesn't aim it at Alina.

Not even once.

Good. They really are loyal to her.

She tilts her head, "I asked you something, didn't I, Fabian?"

He looks at her and lowers his gun slightly. "We know Mr. Moskal is dead."

Alina nods, "Good, we are all on the same page, aren't we?"

She starts walking towards the mansion but then turns back to Fabian.

"And Fabian, please tell your men to lower their guns, will you?"

Fabian nods at his men, and I watch as all of them lower their guns.

I keep my hand on my gun, just in case.

"Furthermore, I require all men to assemble in my father's office. I have a message for all of you." She then turns to Ari and Stian and instructs, "Ari and Stian, I need you to stand guard while I address the men."

As we enter the house, I notice her hands trembling, so I gently place a hand on her shoulder.

Alina looks at me and bites her lip, and I know she's trying to keep it together. I step closer and whisper, so only she can hear me, "It's going to be all right."

She shakes my hand off her shoulder.

I know I deserve it.

"I know you are mad..."

She looks lost and whispers, "I'm scared."

I take her hand and squeeze it gently.

She hesitates but lets me do it.

"You can't show them that. I'll be with you the whole time, gun in hand."

I can feel her grip on my hand tighten as we approach the office. We stand beside each other as the men gather at Nikolai's desk.

Alina clears her throat and begins to speak, "As you all surely know by now, my father is gone. I don't know what details you know or think you know, but what matters is that my father is no longer in charge."

They all keep quiet.

They are all listening to her words.

"Things are going to change around here. The ways you are used to working will change, and you will be informed about those changes in due time. Also, my father's business will keep on going through me, and you will all keep your positions. The guards will keep on guarding, and the dealers will keep on dealing, and so on."

Fabian steps forward, indicating that he wants to talk.

"Fabian," Alina says.

"What do you want to do with your father's body? And how do you want to communicate his passing?"

I don't think she thought about this.

I don't believe she thought she would have to deal with her father's body and funeral arrangements.

"That's something I still have to decide," Alina replies calmly, "Did you retrieve my father's body?"

"We did," Fabian informs.

Alina takes a deep breath, "I need all of you to gather here tomorrow morning. I have some announcements to make about the future of this business, and I expect all of you to be here."

The men nod and start to leave the room.

This is just the beginning...

... and I can already tell it will be a bumpy road.

●

We've been in Nikolai's office, now Alina's office trying to help Alina decide what to do about her father, the communication on his death... *everything*.

His associates will probably try to take advantage of Alina now that Nikolai is gone and she's in charge.

"Okay, let's go through all of this again," Alina says, "Kane will keep on being my bodyguard. Same as before, where I go, you go. I'm sure many people want me dead, now more than ever..." I nod, and she continues, "Stian and Ari, I want you both to be part of this if you really want to. I know you already said yes, but I don't want you guys to feel like you must do it."

"Alina, everything I know is serving the Moskal family, I was here for your father, and I was loyal to him, to a certain point... so I'm here for you, and I'll be loyal to you," Stian says.

"Thank you. I will need your help Stian, a lot... you are used to all my father's businesses, schemes, associates... everything. I know nothing about this, and I know nothing about leadership."

Stian approaches her, "I know you don't. I know you weren't expecting this now, but this day would come, sooner or later... and it came sooner. I know you will be able to do it and cleaner than your father did."

Alina takes a deep breath, "Thank you. I want you to be my counselor."

Stian laughs, "Okay, Miss Moskal."

"Oh no, please... don't call me that."

"Which reminds me," Stian says, "You can't let the men be so personal to you, okay Alina? I know you are used to people calling you by your first name, but now you are in charge... you are Miss Moskal for all the men."

"I don't like that..." Alina complains.

"I am sure you don't, but you'll get used to it."

"Okay, but you three are forbidden from calling me Miss Moskal."

I chuckle, "Would never, princess."

Alina smiles at me, even though she clearly didn't want me to notice it.

"Okay, let's get back to business," she says. "We must decide how to communicate my father's passing to his associates."

"We could send out a formal letter," Ari suggests.

"Or we could make a public announcement," Stian adds.

"No," Alina says firmly. "We can't give them too much information. They already know my father is dead and will try to use that to their advantage. We need to keep things vague."

"What about a coded message?" I suggest. "Something that only the people you trust will be able to understand."

"That's a good idea. We can use a code we know they'll recognize. Something only my father's closest associates would know."

"We'll have to be careful with that," Stian warns. "We don't want the wrong people catching on."

"I know," Alina nods.

We spend the next hour brainstorming ideas and coming up with a plan.

When it's all wrapped up, Alina asks, "Where's Fabian?"

"He's probably with Nikolai's body," Stian replies.

"I need to talk to him and to see my father's body." She turns to me, "Kane, can you come with me?"

177

"Of course," I say, standing up and following her out of the office.

●

I am walking with Alina down the hallway when she suddenly stops and turns to me. "Kane."

I look at her, waiting for her to continue.

"I'm sorry I broke down when you told me about my father."

"You shouldn't be. He was your father, and it's the normal reaction to have," I reply, trying to comfort her.

"I would have done the same thing," she says quietly. "I don't judge you. He tried to kill you. He tortured you... and yes, you were right before. He killed my mom and did many monstrous things, and I would have killed him myself the day we ran away if you didn't tell me not to do it. And that's why I was mad. Because you didn't let me kill him. I was mad because you decided my future for me, not because you killed him. We weren't close even though we lived in the same house. I won't miss him. He was never one of those caring fathers, you know? He didn't want me dead, and that's all. So, Kane, I'm not mad that you killed him. I'm not sad that he died. I just was not prepared to take over, and you made that decision for me."

I nod slowly, "I am sorry for that."

"I know you are," she replies, walking towards me and touching my face.

She leans in and plants a soft kiss on my lips.

"Now, let's get this over with. I really need a shower," she says with a smile.

CHAPTER TWENTY-SIX

Nikolai's body lies in the mansion, lifeless.

Alina stands stoically before the men, staring at her dead father.

I got to admit.

I'm impressed by Alina right now.

I'm surprised at her lack of emotion, but then again, she's been through a lot before I came into the picture.

Maybe all her anger and resentment towards her father keep her from properly grieving.

I stand in the shadows when one of the men asks, "What's next, Alina? Will you take over your father's organization now that he's dead?"

I wouldn't say I like his tone, but I don't intervene.

For now.

Alina's eyes narrow, and the man continues, "You think you can just come in here and take over?"

You can bet she can, asshole.

Alina briefly studies him, takes a deep breath, and replies, "I'm sure you don't actually mean that. We're all just a bit... shaken by everything that's happened recently. Right?"

Alina's gaze is fixed on the man's gaze when Fabian, hands behind his back, steps forward and says, "Shut up, Tate."

Tate doesn't listen and continues, "You killed Nikolai. How do you want people to respect you and follow you? He was a true leader. You are not."

I'm losing my patience.

I step forward, but Alina puts her arm to the side, signaling me not to do anything.

She still doesn't say anything.

"Tate, shut the fuck up. It's not your place to give your input. Alina Moskal is your leader now, and you will accept it whether you like it or not." Fabian says.

Tate laughs and takes his gun, pointing it at Alina.

At the same time, I take out my gun, and Fabian raises his own gun to Tate.

Tate blinks and chuckles, "Of course," he says.

"Don't," Alina tells me, "Lower your gun, Kane."

"Alina..." I start.

She turns to me and repeats, "Lower your gun."

Against my will, I lower my gun, but Fabian doesn't.

I hear a click coming from Tate's gun, and before Tate can do anything else, Fabian shoots.

The shot echoes through the room, and Tate falls to the ground, *lifeless*.

Alina doesn't flinch.

"You didn't have to do that," she says.

"He was a threat," Fabian replies. "And we don't tolerate threats."

Alina nods and turns around, "Clean this up," she orders, her voice cold as ice.

Fabian nods and begins to move the body, and she walks out of the room, having me following her.

•

I take a deep breath as Alina, and I make our way to her room. The mansion is eerily quiet, the only sound being the soft tap of our footsteps against the marble floors.

"You can't avoid death in this sort of business, Alina," I say quietly, breaking the silence. "People will defy you, and you can't let them do it. Your father never did, and you are expected to do the same."

Alina remains quiet for a moment before replying, "I know, Kane. I know what's expected of me. But that doesn't mean I have to like it. It doesn't mean I have to enjoy it."

I nod, "I don't know Fabian very well, but the thing he did... he was right. Tate was a threat, and we can't accept it, especially when you are taking over. You can't show weakness."

Alina turns to me, and I stop in my tracks.

She walks right up to me, stopping inches from my chest.

Her warm breath is against my skin as she looks up at me.

"I am not weak." She says, her lips crashing onto mine.

Alina presses her lips harder against mine without giving me a chance to reply. I feel the heat radiating from her body as she pushes herself against me, and I respond by wrapping my arms around her waist, pulling her even closer to me.

Our lips move in perfect synchronization.

Alina's hands tangle in my hair, pulling me closer to her as she deepens the kiss.

"Alina," I try to speak.

"Shh," she says between the kisses.

Alina's lips are hot and demanding, and I respond eagerly.

My hands roam over her body, feeling the curves and lines of her figure through the fabric of her clothes. Alina moans into my mouth, and without breaking the kiss, I lift her and carry her to her bed.

I lay her down gently, never taking my lips off hers.

Our bodies are pressed together.

The heat is emanating from every inch of her skin.

Alina takes control, pushing me back onto the bed as she straddles me.

She breaks the kiss and looks down at me.

"You're mine, Kane," she whispers, trailing kisses down my neck and chest.

I gasp at the sensation.

I feel my body respond to her touch.

Alina's hands roam over my body, exploring every inch with hunger. She reaches for the hem of my shirt, pulling it off in one swift motion as her lips trail down my chest.

Her hands move to my pants, slowly unbuttoning and pulling them down, revealing my already hard cock.

She takes me in her mouth, and I let out a low growl.

Alina's lips are skilled, and she knows how to tease me. I run my fingers through her hair, holding onto her as she takes me.

But just as I'm about to lose control, Alina stops and climbs back up to straddle me again. She looks down at me with a wicked grin.

"Now it's my turn," she says, lowering herself onto me.

I groan as she takes me in, her tightness surrounding me.

Alina moves her hips in a slow, tantalizing rhythm, her eyes never leaving mine.

"I want you to come for me," she whispers, her nails digging into my chest as she picks up the pace.

I grab onto her hips, thrusting up to meet her, and the sound of our bodies slapping together fills the room.

"Alina," I moan.

"Yes, Kane," she breathes, her pace quickening.

Alina leans forward, her breasts brushing against my chest as she brings her lips to my ear.

"Do you like it when I take control, Kane?" her breath is hot against my skin.

I can only nod.

My words are lost in the pleasure she's giving me.

Alina's hands grip my shoulders as she moves faster, her body bouncing over mine.

She leans back, her hands resting on my thighs as she rides me. I watch in awe as she moves with grace and power, her body glistening with sweat.

Shit, she's driving me crazy like this.

Alina slows her movements, still straddling me, and leans down to kiss me. Our tongues dance together, tasting the sweetness.

"I'm not weak, Kane," she whispers, pulling back to look into my eyes. "And neither are you."

I'm completely under her spell.

I'm unable to speak as she continues moving.

With a mischievous glint in her eye, she shifts her position so she's facing away from me. Her back arched as she rode me in reverse.

Her ass is bouncing up and down on my cock.

I reach forward to grab onto her hips, helping to guide her movements.

"Fuck, Alina," I groan. "You're incredible."

She laughs, tossing her blonde hair over her shoulder.

Alina's movements become faster and more erratic, her body trembling as she reaches her peak. I can feel her walls clenching around me, and I know I'm not far behind.

I grab her hips, urging her on as we approach the edge.

"Come with me, Kane," she whispers.

My body convulses with the force of my orgasm as Alina continues to ride me through it.

We're both panting.

Sweat is slicking our bodies.

Alina collapses onto my chest, her breaths coming in short gasps. I wrap my arms around her, holding her close as we catch our breath.

•

"I never said you were weak," I tell her as I lean against the bathroom sink, hearing the shower running in the background.

"I know you didn't," she replies, her voice slightly muffled by the sound of the water. "But I need everyone to know I'm not."

"Please don't show them how you did it with me," I say with a smirk, even though she can't see it from the other side of the shower door.

Alina chuckles, "I won't."

CHAPTER TWENTY-SEVEN

I stand next to Alina at the graveside. The air is thick with the scent of fresh flowers and the sound of whispered prayers. Our heads are bowed in respect as the casket is lowered into the ground.

Alina is tense, her hand gripping mine tightly.

I feel her fear and anxiety, and I know she's caught up in something much larger than herself.

"Are you okay?" I whisper to her, my eyes still fixed on the ground.

"I'm fine," she replies, "Just...nervous."

I nod, knowing that she's not just talking about the funeral.

As we stand there, surrounded by mourners and figures from the underworld, I can sense the weight of their stares at us.

Whispers and sidelong glances.

Suddenly, a commotion breaks out near the entrance of the cemetery. Alina and I turn to see a group of men in black suits and sunglasses pushing their way through the crowd.

"Who are they?" Alina asks.

"I don't know," I reply, reaching for the gun.

Something isn't right.

The men approach the graveside, their eyes fixed on Alina. One of them steps forward, a smirk on his lips.

"Alina, my dear," he says, "I'm sorry for your loss."

Alina's face is stony as she looks at him. "Who are you?"

The man laughs. "Oh, just a friend of the family," I can see the menace in his eyes as he speaks.

Another group of men appears, wearing the same black suits and sunglasses. They move towards us, their hands reaching for their holsters.

"Get down!" I shout to Alina, pulling her to the ground as gunfire echoes through the cemetery.

The mourners scatter in all directions.

They scream.

They cry.

There are a lot of Nikolai men here.

Some of them have done some pretty messed up things.

But, on the flip side, plenty of innocent folks are mixed in.

A lot of innocent people are dying here today.

Alina and I huddle behind a gravestone, watching the rival factions fight for control.

"This is madness," Alina whispers.

"I know," I reply.

The crackle of gunfire fills the air.

The acrid smell of gunpowder invades my nostrils.

Bullets whiz past us, striking tombstones and sending shards of marble flying. I keep Alina close, shielding her with my body, as we remain hidden behind the gravestone.

"We have to find a way out of here," I say, "Can you run?"

Alina nods.

We wait for a lull in the gunfire, then break for it, darting from one cover to another. The cemetery is a maze of chaos and destruction, but we navigate it using headstones and trees as shields.

As we approach the cemetery's exit, we encounter pockets of resistance.

Our adversaries are relentless, determined to eliminate anyone who stands in their way.

I fight back, returning fire when necessary.

I need to rely on my training and instincts to survive.

"Stay close to me," I shout over the sound of gunshots, my voice barely audible amidst the chaos.

Alina nods, and her grip on my hand tightens.

A figure emerges from the smoke, blocking our path.

Stian...

"You need to get out of here. The situation has spiraled out of control."

"But we can't just leave," Alina protests.

"I know, but it's not safe. We'll regroup and figure out our next move," Stian says.

Alina looks at me, her eyes pleading for me to find a way out of this, and I take a deep breath, trying to think clearly amidst the chaos.

"We need a distraction," I say, "Something to throw them off our trail."

Stian nods. "I can create a diversion. You two make a run for it."

He disappears into the smoke, and we watch as he engages the enemy, drawing their attention away from us.

"Now!" I shout, grabbing Alina's hand and sprinting towards the exit.

We dodge bullets and leap over obstacles, our hearts pounding in our chests.

We burst through the cemetery gate into the relative safety of the street.

I scan the area.

I need to make sure we're not being followed.

"Come on," I say, pulling Alina toward a nearby alleyway.

We duck into the narrow passage, the sounds of gunfire slowly fading away.

Alina slumps against the wall, her breathing heavy.

"That was insane," she says, her voice shaking.

I nod, trying to catch my breath. "We need to keep moving. We're not safe yet."

We walk through the old buildings.

There are graffiti scrawled across their walls.

The pavement is cracked and littered with debris.

"We need to find somewhere to lay low for a while," I say.

Alina looks at me, "Do you have somewhere in mind?"

I shake my head. "Not yet, but we can't stay out in the open like this. We'll be sitting ducks."

We continue down the alley, our steps slow and cautious.

We are in the middle of a turf war between two powerful factions. *We don't know who to trust or who to turn to.*

They are all supposed to be loyal to Alina as they were to Nikolai, but this outcome was already expected, even though we're not sure what they're fighting over.

We turn a corner and come face to face with a group of men.

Shit.

We are fucked.

I reach for my gun, but one of the men steps forward before I can pull it out.

"We've been looking for you," he says.

My heart pounds in my chest as I try to gauge their intentions.

"What do you want?" I ask, my hand still hovering near my weapon.

"We're not here to hurt you," the man says. "We're here to help."

Alina and I exchange a look.

I bet she is as skeptical as I am.

"Why should we trust you?" Alina asks.

The man steps closer, "Because we have a common enemy," he says. "And we need to work together if we're going to survive."

I take a deep breath, trying to keep my emotions in check. "Who's this common enemy?" I ask.

The man pauses for a moment as if considering his words. "The Serranos," he says finally.

The Serranos are one of the factions we just escaped from.

They only respected Nikolai out of fear.

Without Nikolai, there's no fear.

Without Nikolai, there's no control over them.

"Why should we believe you?" I ask.

"The Serranos are out for blood and won't stop until they get it. I don't think you have much of a choice." He says.

And he is right.

We don't.

CHAPTER TWENTY-EIGHT

"I'm Ivan," the man says, echoing through the dimly lit alleyway.

I keep Alina close behind me without a word as we follow Ivan and his men through the winding paths. The sound of our footsteps resonates through the narrow streets, and the flickering light of the occasional streetlamp casts eerie shadows on the walls.

I don't trust these guys...

... but we don't have much of a choice.

"We were one of Nikolai's trusted allies," Ivan continues, his gaze fixed ahead, "we owe him a debt, so we will protect his legacy by protecting you."

"What do you suggest we do?" I ask.

"We have a safe house on the city's outskirts," Ivan says, "It's heavily guarded and secure. We can keep you there until you decide what to do."

"I know what to do." Alina finally speaks.

Do you?

"You do?" I ask.

"Yes. I can't show fear. You were the one who said it, Kane. I am supposed to lead, and they are supposed to respect me and follow me like they followed my father."

"What's your plan?" I ask.

"How much do you owe my father?" Alina asks Ivan.

"A lot." He simply answers.

"Enough to capture one of the Serranos while my men are busy fighting with them?"

What is she thinking?

"They know what they are doing, right? They know what to expect from my men but don't know what to expect from yours." Alina explains, her voice steady.

"That puts my men in danger," Ivan says.

"You just said you owe my family."

"I don't owe your family. I owe Nikolai."

"No. As you said before, I'm his legacy. You owe me." Alina doesn't blink, her eyes fixed on Ivan.

•

Ivan takes the black hood off the man's head, revealing his face. He's a younger guy, maybe in his mid-twenties, with a face that looks like it's seen a few too many fights.

He glares at us from behind the duct tape that covers his mouth.

Alina signals for Ivan and his men to leave. They nod and file out of the warehouse, leaving us alone.

The man struggles against the ropes that bind him to the chair, but they're tight. He looks at Alina with anger in his eyes.

Alina approaches him, "You know why you're here?"

The man stares at her, his eyes blazing with defiance.

I step forward. "Answer her," I say, my voice low.

The man turns his head and looks at me, his eyes narrowing. He says something, but it's muffled by the tape over his mouth.

Alina rips the tape off quickly, causing the man to flinch. "Speak," she says.

The man spits out a wad of saliva and blood. "Go to hell," he snarls.

I step forward and grab him by the throat. "Answer her," I repeat, my grip tightening.

The man struggles against my grip.

I don't let go.

"Because of the attack," he finally chokes out.

I release the man, and he gasps for air, coughing and spluttering.

Alina takes a step closer to the man, her gaze unyielding. "Who ordered the attack?"

The man glares at her, "I don't answer to you."

"You will answer to me," she says. "You and your comrades attacked us, and you failed. You thought you could take out Nikolai's daughter, but you were wrong."

She steps away from him.

"Your boss, Hector, needs to know that he can't mess with us," Alina continues. "He needs to know that he can't just attack us and get away with it."

I raise an eyebrow.

Alina turns to me, "Kane, I want to use him to send a message."

"What kind of message?" I ask, still trying to figure out where she's going with this.

"I want to show the Serranos they need to respect me," Alina says, "I want to show them that they can't just attack us and get away with it. And I want to use him to do it."

I look at the man, still tied to the chair, his eyes fixed on Alina. "What do you have in mind?"

"I want to send him back to them," Alina says. "But not before we've shown him what happens when you mess with the wrong people."

Is that excitement in her eyes?

There's no stopping her now.

She's determined to show the Serranos she's not to be messed with.

"And what do you want me to do?" I ask.

"I want you to make sure he gets back to the Serranos in one piece," Alina says. "But first, I want you to make an example of him. Show him what happens when you cross us."

"And how do you want me to do that?"

Alina walks over to a nearby table and picks up a hammer.

She turns back to the man and raises the hammer above her head.

"Alina, what are you doing?" I ask, my voice rising.

She pauses for a moment, looking at me. "Sending a message."

With one swift movement, she brings the hammer down on the man's hand, crushing his fingers. The man screams, his body convulsing in pain.

I step forward, trying to intervene, but Alina holds up a hand to stop me.

"We're not finished yet," she says, a cold glint in her eyes.

I watch as she raises the hammer again and brings it down on the man's other hand.

He screams again, *louder this time*.

"Enough," I say, stepping forward.

Alina drops the hammer onto the table.

Her chest is heaving with exertion.

"Ivan will take him back to the Serranos," she says.

I can't believe what I've just witnessed.

I never saw Alina doing something like this.

The Serranos need to know that we mean business...

... but through her hands?

I saw Nikolai in her for a second, *and I'm not sure I liked it*.

I nod, wordlessly acknowledging her plan.

"Actually," she pauses mid-sentence, "you and I will do it together. If we're going to send a message, we'll do it face to face."

CHAPTER TWENTY-NINE

ALINA

I watch Kane as he dials Stian's number and puts the phone to his ear. I can't hear what Stian is saying on the other end, so I look at Kane as he speaks, brushing his hair back with the hand, not holding the phone.

I turn my attention to the man tied in the chair.

At his bloody broken hands.

I enjoyed what I did to him.

It feels good to have power.

It feels good to do things I never thought I would.

Kane ends the call, "Stian is okay. Many people went down during the shooting, but Stian is coming with more of your men to give us a ride to the Serrano's place."

"Good," I say, approaching Kane.

He doesn't move.

He is looking at me differently.

I reach for his face, planting a kiss on his lips.

He doesn't kiss me back.

"What?" I ask.

Kane semi-closes his eyes and presses his lips together. "Nothing," he says and walks past me to approach the guy on the chair, taking some tape and putting it over the man's mouth.

"What, Kane?" I repeat.

Still crouching in front of the guy, Kane moves his head to face me and gets up. He walks to me and pulls me to the corner of the room, whispering. "I didn't recognize you there, Alina. That's all."

I take my arm away from his grip and reply, "You were the one who said I couldn't show fear."

Kane chuckles and replies, "You went from not showing fear to someone who breaks hands pretty quickly, don't you think?"

I can't believe he is attacking me with that.

"Because you did such pretty things while working for my father, didn't you?"

Kane rubs his face with his hand and says, "The difference is I was indeed working for your father, but you are looking like him."

I can feel my blood boil at his words. "What does that even mean?" I ask, my voice rising.

Kane sighs and shakes his head. "Alina... Come one."

How could he say that to me?

I'm not my father.

I'm not a monster.

I'm just trying to survive.

I thought Kane understood that.

"You think I'm like him?" I ask.

Kane shakes his head, " I just meant that you're starting to enjoy this too much. It's not healthy."

I take a step back, "I'm nothing like him."

Kane looks at me momentarily before saying, "I hope you're right."

I watch as he walks outside, leaving me alone with the guy tied to the chair.

I try to push Kane's words out of my mind...

...but they keep creeping back in.

Am I becoming like my father?

•

We arrive at the Serrano's place.

This place is like a fortress.

Men with guns surround us as we step out of the car. Stian and Kane have their guns in place, and the rest of my men follow suit.

The tension in the air is palpable as we make our way through the heavily guarded entrance.

Kane takes the guy from the car and shoves him to the floor.

I step forward, feeling the eyes of the Serrano men on me.

I take a deep breath and stand tall.

I'm ready to show them who Alina Moskal is.

"I'm here to talk to Hector Serrano," I say, my voice steady.

One of the Serrano men steps forward, a sneer on his face. "And who are you, little girl?" he says, his hand on his gun.

"Tell Hector Alina Moskal is here. Now."

The man laughs, and I take a step forward.

"Listen to me," I say, my voice rising. "I'm not here to play games. You will show me respect, or there will be consequences."

Hector Serrano himself steps forward, a grin on his face. "Well, well, well. Look at you, all grown up and playing gangster. Tell me, Alina, what makes you think you can come here and demand respect?"

"Because I have more men than you do, Hector. And if you don't show me the respect I deserve, I will order my men to start shooting."

Hector laughs. "You wouldn't dare," he says.

I smile coldly. "Oh, I would. And I will. Unless you and your men swear loyalty to me right now."

Hector hesitates. I raise my hand, signaling to my men to get ready.

"Last chance, Hector," I say, my voice hard. "Swear loyalty to me, or face the consequences."

Hector chuckles, and one of his men lifts his gun. As soon as the gunshot echoes through the room, my eyes dart to Kane, who is already raising his weapon and firing without hesitation.

The Serrano's man falls to the ground, lifeless.

I turn my gaze back to Hector, who looks shaken but defiant. "If I were you, I would start talking," I say, my voice low and menacing.

Hector just sneers. "Never!"

"Very well," I say, nodding to one of my men.

He steps forward and aims at one of Hector's men.

The Serrano's men all raise their guns, causing all my men to do the same.

Stian quickly steps forward and aims, causing the Serrano's men to falter. Kane keeps his gun pointed at the fallen man's body, making sure no one else makes a move.

"DON'T," Hector yells to his men.

Hector hesitates for a moment.

His eyes flicker between me and my men.

Finally, he gives a reluctant nod. "Fine."

Hector," I take a deep breath, "you made the right choice."

Hector doesn't flinch.

I step closer to him, my gaze locked on his. "Now, I want you to do something for me, Hector."

"What do you want?"

"I want you to kneel," I smile. "You think I'm going to kneel to you?" he says, raising his voice.

I raise my hand, signaling my men to prepare for sudden moves.

"Yes, Hector. I think you're going to kneel to me. Or do you want to see more of your men fall?"

Hector glares at me for a moment before reluctantly dropping to his knees.

"Good," I say, pleased with his compliance clapping my hands. "Now, swear your undying loyalty to me, Hector. And don't forget who's in charge here."

Hector grinds his teeth together before speaking. "I swear my undying loyalty to you, Alina Moskal."

"Very good. You may stand." I smile, satisfied with my dominance.

As Hector rises to his feet, I turn to my men. "Let's go. We have work to do."

The tension in the air dissipates as we leave the Serrano's fortress.

I feel the power surging through my veins.

With Hector's allegiance, I am one step closer to total control.

But I also know that this is just the beginning.

The road ahead will be dangerous...

But then again, I am ready for whatever comes my way.

Because I am Alina Moskal...

... and I am not to be underestimated.

CHAPTER THIRTY

ALINA

We arrive at the mansion, and Kane strides ahead, not looking back.

"Stian, do you have a second to talk?" I ask.

I feel a lump forming in my throat.

I need guidance.

I need someone to tell me that I'm doing the right thing.

"Of course, Alina," Stian replies calmly.

"I don't know how to deal with this," I confess. "If I try to lead, I'm afraid I'll end up looking like my father. I don't want to be a monster."

"You don't have to be Nikolai to lead. Yes, you need to be fearless, but that doesn't mean you must be cold-blooded like your father. You can lead with empathy, with kindness, with compassion. You can be a different kind of leader who inspires people instead of ruling them with an iron fist."

I take a deep breath, trying to absorb Stian's words.

He's right, of course.

I don't have to be like my father to be a strong leader.

I can carve my own path and create my own legacy.

"What about Kane?" I ask, gesturing toward his retreating figure. "He's acting so differently now."

Stian follows my gaze and nods. "Kane will always remain loyal to you, no matter what you do. It's up to you to decide what kind of relationship you want to have with him. If you follow in your father's footsteps..." he pauses for a second, "Knowing Kane, I know he will be nothing more than your bodyguard."

I don't want Kane to be just my bodyguard.

I give Stian a small smile, and we enter the mansion.

I'm not my father.

I'm not a monster.

I take a deep breath and head to Kane's room, my heart pounding in my chest. As I push open the door, I see Kane putting his gun away in his desk drawer.

"Kane, can we talk?" I ask softly.

He looks up, and his expression doesn't betray anything. "Of course."

I close the door behind me and walk over to him.

"Kane, I don't want to be like my father," I say, my voice shaky. "And I don't want to lose you."

Kane raises an eyebrow. "Looks like you're enjoying it too much already."

I shake my head. "I don't want to enjoy it. I need your help. I can't do this alone."

He looks at me for a moment before speaking. "Alina, you know I'll be loyal to you and protect you no matter what you do. You don't have to worry about that."

He walks past me, but I stop him by pulling his arm, making him look me in the eyes.

"Kane, I love you. Don't do this to me, please," I plead.

He doesn't say anything for a minute, leaving nothing but silence in the room.

"I'm not doing anything," he finally says.

"I don't want to be another Nikolai Moskal," I whisper. "I want to do things differently."

Kane doesn't respond, so I get closer to him.

"Please, Kane," I say, my voice barely audible. "I need you."

He finally looks at me.

I see conflict in his eyes.

"Kane, you don't get it. You're not just my bodyguard. You're my anchor, my confidant. You ground me and remind me of the person I want to be. If I lose you, I'm afraid I'll lose myself too."

His eyes pierce into mine. "You won't lose me, Alina. I've dedicated myself to protecting you and don't intend to abandon you now. But you need to understand I can't make your choices for you. I can guide you, but ultimately, it's your responsibility to shape your own path."

"I know," I whisper, "I won't let the darkness consume me. I believe I can create a different legacy with you by my side. Different from my father's one."

He takes a deep breath and leans in, his lips finding mine.

Kane's lips press against mine with an intensity that matches the storm of emotions swirling inside me. His hands reach my waist, pulling me closer as our bodies meld together.

I thread my fingers through his hair, pulling him impossibly closer as the intensity of the kiss deepens. Our bodies press against each other.

At this moment, there is no darkness.

There is no uncertainty.
The kiss slowly comes to an end, and we pull away.
"Kane, I..." I start talking, but he interrupts me.
"Don't say anything," he says, touching my lips.
I don't know what the future holds.
But I know one thing...
With Kane by my side, I can face anything.

EPILOGUE

KANE

I can't believe it's been a year since Alina took over her father's empire.

It's been a whirlwind of power plays.

Of betrayals.

Of bloodshed.

But it's also been a year of growth, of learning what it truly means to be a leader.

I stand on the balcony, watching the lights twinkle in the darkness.

Alina's come a long way, and even though she tries not to be her father, in this type of world, it isn't always possible.

She has become someone strong...

Someone feared...

Someone respected.

But at what cost?

She has also become someone who orders executions...

Someone who makes deals with the devil.

But honestly?

I can't even blame her.

I made this choice for her...

If I hadn't killed her father, she wouldn't be in charge of the Moskal business.

She wouldn't have to deal with all of this.

The road ahead is dark and dangerous.

But we are not afraid.

We've faced worse.

I turn away from the balcony and head back inside.

As I enter the room, I find Alina sitting at her desk, staring intently at the computer screen.

"Anything interesting?" I ask, taking a seat on the couch.

She looks up at me, her eyes tired.

"Just business as usual," she replies, her voice flat.

I can tell she's exhausted.

Leading Moskal's empire is not an easy job.

But she's doing it.

"You know, we don't have to do this forever," I say, "we can leave this life behind and start over."

Alina looks at me, surprised.

"Start over?" she repeats.

"Yeah. We can go somewhere far away from all of this. Live a simple life."

But Alina shakes her head, "I can't just abandon everything."

I nod.

Alina's phone rings, and she answers it.

I can hear the tension in her voice as she talks.

"Meet me at the warehouse," she says before hanging up.

I stand up, ready to go with her, but Alina stops me.

"No, Kane. This one is mine. I need to do this alone."

"I'm coming with you."

"No, you are not." She tells me.

I take a deep breath before agreeing. "Be careful," I say, watching her leave the room.

She disappears down the hallway, and I can't help but worry about what she's getting herself into.

But I also know that she's a force to be reckoned with.

Alina Moskal is a leader.

And I'm proud to stand by her side.

•

THE END

ACKNOWLEGEMENTS

Writing this book has been an incredibly special journey for me, filled with ups and downs, moments of doubt, and moments of pure inspiration. It is with great joy and gratitude that I express my heartfelt thanks to those who have played a significant role in bringing this book to life.

First and foremost, I want to express my deepest appreciation to my mom, who has been a constant pillar of support and encouragement throughout my writing journey. Your unwavering belief in me and your endless words of encouragement have given me the strength and confidence to pursue my passion, even when doubts crept in. **Thank you for always being there, Mom, and for being the one constant presence in the acknowledgments section of all my books.**

To my boyfriend, who lovingly teases me about writing "porn" even though this book is filled with action and violence, thank you for your unwavering support and understanding. Your playful banter and unwavering belief in my abilities have been a source of inspiration and motivation. Your presence in my life fuels my creativity, and I am grateful for your love and encouragement.

I would also like to extend my heartfelt gratitude to **Maria Santos** (@mariasstoriesinamovie on Instagram) for her unwavering support and invaluable contributions to my growth as a writer and author. Maria, thank you for being a trusted beta reader for this book and for providing invaluable feedback and suggestions that have shaped its final form. Your dedication to helping me become the best writer I can be is immeasurable, and your assistance will forever be treasured.

A special thank you goes out to all the **bookstagrammers** and readers who have embraced my work and supported me along this writing journey. Your enthusiasm, reviews, and kind words have meant the world to me. It is your belief in my stories that keep me motivated to continue writing and sharing my imagination with the world.

To all those mentioned and countless others who have contributed to this book in ways big and small, thank you from the bottom of my heart. Your presence in my life and in the creation of this story is deeply appreciated, and I am forever grateful for the role you have played.

ABOUT THE AUTHOR

Frances Blackthorn is a European author with a passion for coffee and animals, particularly her beloved black cat.

Frances has been an avid romance reader since her teenage years, devouring all types of romance novels, from Young Adult to Adult and everything in between. She has a particular fondness for Enemies to Lovers and dark romance stories.

When she's not lost in a book or crafting her own stories, Frances works as a trademark paralegal at an Intellectual Property office in southern Europe.

Despite her demanding 8 hour job, Frances makes time for her true passion: reading and writing. She believes that there's nothing quite like getting lost in a good book or creating worlds and characters of her own.

For more from Frances:
Visit her website at www.francesblackthorn.com
Follow her on Instagram (@francesblackthorn)

ALSO BY FRANCES BLACKTHORN

If you enjoy clean romances, check the **Under Seattle's Sky** series:

Book 1: Trade Secret of a Messy Relationship
Book 2: This Little Thing Called Love
Book 3: *to be released*

If you enjoy spicy and quick romances, check the **Shadows of Seduction** series:

Book 1: Corrupted by Sin
Book 2: *to be released*

Milton Keynes UK
Ingram Content Group UK Ltd.
UKHW010800150823
426904UK00004B/352

9 798890 749031